GREER AND REMI: A RED TEAM WEDDING NOVELLA

RED TEAM, BOOK 15

ELAINE LEVINE

Published by Elaine Levine
Copyright © 2019 Elaine Levine
Last Updated: October 27, 2019
Cover art by The Killion Group, Inc.
Editing by Arran McNicol @ editing720
Proofing by Jenn @ SideKickJenn.com
Proofing by Stephanie @ Enterprise Book Services

GREER AND REMI: A RED TEAM WEDDING NOVELLA

RED TEAM, BOOK 15

Dr. Remington Chase is finally ready to fulfill a promise she made to herself more than a decade earlier: confront the Grummonds and demand they release her mother's body into her custody. She tried and failed earlier in a quest that wrecked her world and brought her to the attention of a group of terrorists...and one particular assassin hunting them: Greer Dawson.

This time, with Greer by her side, she learns the polygamist community that stole her childhood has crumbled from the inside out. A new secular town government has been put in place, and its mayor is more than happy to help Remi resolve the mystery of her mother's resting place.

It isn't until Greer's family comes to Wolf Creek Bend for a reunion that the truth of Remi's mother's death is finally revealed—a truth so devastating that it might derail their spontaneous wedding plans.

Length: Approximately 150 pages
Ages: 18 & up (story contains adult situations and profanity)

Greer and Remi: A Red Team Wedding Novella (The Red Team, Book 15) is part of a serialized story that includes nine full-length novels and nine wedding novellas. This series is best read in order, starting with The Edge of Courage.

Join the conversation on Facebook: Visit Elaine Levine's War Room - http://geni.us/hxFk to talk about this book and all of her suspenseful stories!

SLEEPER SEALS

ROMANTIC SUSPENSE/MILITARY SUSPENSE

MEN OF DEFIANCE SERIES

HISTORICAL WESTERN ROMANCE

(This series may be read in any order.)

DEDICATION

Barry—
I've written many wedding stories, from spontaneous events to
intricately planned ceremonies, celebrations that took place in
harem tents and decorated basketball courts, but the best I've
ever experienced was the real-life one featuring you.

1

The stack of student exams Remi still needed to grade hadn't gotten much smaller, despite the extra hours she'd been putting in over the last few days. Her office was on the north side of the building, so it was generally dark, but she was surprised how late it was. The afternoon had rolled past dusk and was well into evening. A knot settled in her stomach; she knew better than to be out this time of day—and so far from home.

She supposed she should head out while there were still people around campus. She gathered up her tests to grade and snapped an oversized rubber band around the stack, then slipped them into her briefcase. She shut off her desk light. Before she could step out of her small office, she saw Greer leaning against the wall opposite her door out in the hallway. His hands were shoved in his jeans pockets and his eyes looked wrecked.

How long had he been there? And what had upset him?

She set her briefcase down, then crossed the hall, grabbed a fistful of his sheepskin coat and dragged him back into her office. He kicked the door shut behind him and wrapped his heavy arms around her. Their first kiss was long and intense, as if they hadn't seen each other in weeks rather than just since the morning.

Greer was the first to pull back. "Hi."

She moved her hands from around his neck to wrap them around his waist. "Sorry I'm here so late."

"I have some news that I didn't want to wait to tell you about."

"What kind of news?" Greer was an intense guy even when he was laughing, but somber like this, he straight-up gave her the willies.

"We got the court order for you to take custody of your mom's body. We can go get her tomorrow, if you can take some leave."

Remi's lungs skipped a breath. She was glad she'd had Greer be her point of contact; he had more availability during the day to chase this down. And this way, he'd be with her when any news came in. "Colorado authorized her disinterment?"

"Yes and no."

"Greer—a straight answer, please."

"Because the Grummond Society never filed for a death certificate and didn't get an interment permit, we don't exactly have proof that they have her body."

"What about the letters I received from my mom's

friends inside the community?"

Greer nodded. "Those letters are what finally enabled a court to demand we be given access to her grave. It requires the Grummonds to escort us to your mom's grave and allows us to disinter her. The problem is that we don't know for sure how or where they disposed of her body. They may have had her cremated. But at least we can go find out what happened." He gave her a measuring look. "Are you up to this? I can do it on your behalf, if you'd rather."

"No. I've wanted to know what happened to her ever since she went back. I'll put a call in to my department head to get the next few days of my classes covered."

Greer gave her an odd, tense smile. "I have more info. I've gotten clearance to take your spring break week off with you next month. I'd like to bring my parents and sisters and their husbands out to meet you."

"Oh."

"Oh?"

"Do you think we should?"

"Is there a reason we shouldn't?"

"Do they know about me? I mean, about my past?"

"I haven't told them about your background, only who you are now. They've been antsy to meet you." He gave her a rueful grin. "I get the feeling they think you're way above my pay grade."

"What does that mean?"

"I think they're surprised I landed a smart, ambitious, gorgeous woman with an exciting career."

"Why would that surprise them? You're all of those things yourself—except the woman part."

His eyes grew somber. "I don't think they expected me to live this long. They don't really have a handle on what I do. They still think it's something shady."

"Well, it kind of is."

"True."

"All right. Let's do it." She frowned. "We need to get their trip planned. Tickets will get expensive if we wait too long."

"We have Owen's plane. No tickets needed." Greer's grin was blinding. "I might see if my sisters can send their kids to family that week. I don't want to over-whelm you."

"I hope they do bring the kids. I love kids—they wouldn't overwhelm me."

Greer lifted his brows. "You love kids?"

"Yeah."

His cheeks reddened. She had a flash of insight as she imagined he was thinking about starting their family. Her own cheeks warmed. She giggled a little. "Have you let Ace and Val know? I hope they can clear their sched-ules too."

"That okay with you?"

"They're family, Greer. Of course it is. Besides, while Ace reconnected with your parents a while ago, she hasn't had a chance to meet up with your sisters. There's a whole other half of your family she still needs to bond with. And it's good for your family to get to know Val as well."

Greer blew out a long breath. "As much as I want my family to meet you, I also don't want to share you. I want you all to myself, a week in bed with you."

Remi felt the heat in Greer's blazing eyes. Maybe she needed to make a quick shopping trip, pick up some lingerie to drive him crazy—she was sure they could carve out some time alone during their vacation. "This is going to be a fun visit."

"It will. But first, things are going to be emotional while we retrieve your mom."

She grabbed her things and followed him into the hallway, locking her door behind her. "Do you think we're safe to do this? The last time I went down there, all hell broke loose."

His warm, whiskey-colored eyes hardened. "Last time you didn't have me."

Remi suppressed a shiver, glad she wasn't on the receiving end of his ferocity. Remi slipped her hand in his as they went down her hall and into the stairwell.

Greer opened the outside door at the ground floor. A cold blast of air blew around them. The campus lights were on, brightening the walkways. Remi sent a nervous glance around. She saw Greer's big black SUV parked next to her Forester.

Her car was under a tall streetlight, a spot she'd chosen on purpose. She didn't miss how Greer checked it out when she unlocked it. She got in and locked it, then gave him a quick smile.

Life had gotten so unexpectedly complicated, but having Greer near always made her feel safe.

2

The drive from Wolf Creek Bend down to the little town in southwestern Colorado where the Grummond Society was situated took close to ten hours. Though they'd gotten on the road before dawn, it was late afternoon before they arrived.

Blanco Ridge was in a long and narrow valley framed by cliffs of beige sandstone. In its heyday, the sect was home to some two thousand adherents. The group began its decline more than a dozen years ago, when its leader, Esrom Stanton, died. The Prophet Josiah — Senator Whiddon — had loosely taken the reins at the time. But the demands on his time in Washington, D.C., had meant he had to appoint junior leaders. None of them had been able to keep the group together. They'd used their sudden rise to power as an opportunity to harvest the group for their twisted proclivities. The town slowly fell to their ruthlessness. And when

Senator Whiddon had died a few months ago, it all fell apart.

Currently, the group was being heavily investigated. Several leaders were charged with tax fraud, real estate fraud, child endangerment, and sex trafficking.

Remi hadn't kept in contact with anyone from the Society. The people her mom had corresponded with hadn't written any letters after letting her know that her mom had passed away.

Remi was uncertain what they were driving into as they hit the outskirts of the town. She closed her eyes and took a few calming breaths, envisioning the outcome she wanted rather than the one she feared.

The SUV slowed down as Greer made a turn. "We're here," he said.

Though she tried, no amount of deep breathing could calm her rising panic. She opened her eyes, expecting the compound's security to block their way.

None did.

Whatever she'd imagined, it wasn't anything like what they saw. The place was a ghost town. There was a cluster of families—mostly women—living in converted shipping containers in what had once been a community pasture. Horses in nearby corrals were thin. Abandoned dogs were running in packs.

Houses that had always been tidy when she was a kid now looked like survivors of multiple earthquakes. Windows were broken, shutters hung askew; front doors were open or missing, exposing trashed interiors. Guilt stabbed through her. For so many years, she'd wanted to see the Society destroyed. And it looked like it had been, but nothing had shored up the lives of those left behind.

Greer drove down the main street in town. A few places were open for business: a post office, an old diner, a town hall, hardware and grocery stores. Some of those were things she didn't recognize. Town business had generally been run out of some of the small cottages along the main street. There hadn't been a post office because the community had never incorporated and had no established relationship with the county, state, or federal governments. The church had owned the whole area, so it was considered private property.

"Turn left," Remi told Greer. "That was my house." She pointed to the little cottage where she and her mother had lived until her mom got them both out. It hadn't escaped the ravages that the rest of the town suffered. Someone had painted it yellow at one time, but the sun had bleached it to a pale cream.

"I'd heard, after Whiddon's death, that the town had begun to fall apart, but this is far worse than I expected."

Greer paused outside her former home. "Whatever happened here, it began a long while ago. The town is too far gone for the destruction to be only months old."

"The church property was put into a trust to benefit remaining residents, but that doesn't seem to be helping anyone left here."

He drove away. "Let's go check in with the B&B, then we can find the town hall and meet the mayor."

The Prophet's B&B had once been Esrom Stanton's property. Prophet Josiah had inherited it. So many terrible things had happened there, all under the guise of building the holy estate of Stanton and Josiah.

The closer they got to the sprawling mansion, the bigger the pit in Remi's stomach grew. Women never entered those hallowed halls without being changed —forever.

Greer drove through the estate's open wrought-iron gates and parked in the designated area. He didn't immediately shut the car off or get out. Both of them looked at the house. "We don't have to stay here. I brought camping gear for backup."

Remi didn't unbuckle her seatbelt. She stared out the window at the imposing building. Part industrial complex, part turreted castle—it wasn't even a pretty structure. "I understand the psychology of having a big white mansion surrounded by a formidable wall in a town of little cottages. I understand, academically, the caste system the Grummonds forced on its membership. I get it. And yet, being here, I feel like a fourteen-year-old girl who's going to be raped by a creepy old man until she's been impregnated."

Greer shook his head. The muscles in his cheeks bunched. He put the SUV in reverse. "Screw this shit. We're outta here."

She stopped him. "No. We're doing this."

"Fuck. It. All. Remi, some stuff isn't cathartic. It's straight-up toxic."

"This is cathartic. This property was purchased from

the church trustees by an apostate who'd left the group when they wouldn't let him marry the woman he loved. They ran away together. She came back after a few hard months and ended up marrying an elderly first cousin. I was still here when all of that happened. Having this place owned and used by those the Society stepped on is vindication."

Greer's eyes held hers as he considered what she'd said. He parked again, then gave her a worried look. "We'll give it a go. But if at any point it's overwhelming for you, we'll find a spot to camp."

She knew the smile she gave him was less than convincing, but this was something she was determined to do.

They walked up to the door and knocked. A dark-haired guy opened the door and greeted them with a big smile. "Hey! You must be Greer and Remi."

They stepped inside the grand foyer. Remi looked around. She'd never been inside before, but she'd heard so many rumors about its ornate decor. The inn's proprietor, Abel, was watching her.

"You're from here, aren't you?" he asked Remi.

She tore her eyes from the paneled walls. It seemed strangely bare without art and antiques filling the space. "I am. My mom got us out a long time ago."

"You and everyone like you—you're why I opened this place. It holds a place in our minds like Fort Knox —impossible to get in or out of. But really, it's just a big house. Why don't I show you around?"

"We'd love a tour," Greer said, "but right now your

new mayor is waiting to meet with us. Maybe we could do that tour tonight or tomorrow?"

"You bet. Just come grab me. I'll show you up to your room. The dining room has an open snack bar. There's a Keurig with all the fixings. Help yourselves at any time."

"Thank you," Remi said. She was filled with questions for him. Had he run into his former girlfriend? Was he enjoying being back? Was the B&B working out well? The town was so far from the beaten path; people had to make an effort to come here, and probably only those who'd once lived in the Society would do that.

Greer brought their things up to their room. It was spacious—the two queen-sized beds didn't overwhelm the space. There was still room for a small love seat, coffee table, dresser, and TV.

He pulled her close and smiled as he looked into her eyes. "Will this do for a night or two?"

She nodded. "It looks more like a regular hotel room than a house of torture. Abel's done a great job."

"And I'm not leaving your side while we're here."

Remi ran her palms up the outside of his beefy arms. He was ripped everywhere she touched. "Thank you. For being here. For everything."

"It's important to me that you get some closure on this."

"Me too."

"Let's go find the mayor. She's waiting for us."

Back outside, they drove a few blocks over, then pulled into a freshly paved parking lot in front of a brick rambler that had been converted into the town hall offices. Some loose dogs barked at them. Greer reached for her hand as they stepped in front of the big SUV. He opened the door for her. A woman called out to them from an office in what looked to once have been a dining room.

"Dr. Chase, I presume?" The woman came over with a warm smile and her hand extended.

"I am. Mayor Sullivan, this is Greer Dawson."

"Just call me Ester," the mayor said. "We're not formal here."

Introductions completed, Ester returned to her desk. Cardboard boxes and plastic bins were stacked along the edges of the room. "I really appreciate your heads-up about your visit," she said. "As you can see, I've gotten custody of years of Grummond Society files. Took me a while to find the ledger our former church clerk kept." She handed a wide, canvas-bound notebook to Remi and gestured toward the two chairs in front of her desk. "There's an entry for every birth, one for every death, then several different ledgers that were used to list church member crimes, punishments, restitutions, and reinstatements."

Ester looked regretful. "You said your mom died here some thirteen years ago. I've not be able to find her death listed. In fact, I can't find any record of her return. But that time period was chaos. The community lost Father Esrom that year. I'm afraid our recordkeeping suffered from all that happened."

"I sent you copies of the letters I received from our

friends still inside the community. They all mentioned her passing," Remi said. "Were you able to find any of those people to question them?"

"I'm afraid not. Before Stanton died, we had over two thousand people living here. We're down to less than five hundred now. Your mother's sister wives have left and/or passed away. The friends who wrote those letters are long gone. Many take on new identities after leaving here. I don't know where they went or who they became. I'm trying to get word out to the former community that it would be safe to return now that we're under state guardianship, but so far that message isn't reaching the ones who most need to hear it. And most of them have deep-rooted fear of any government, so being in a protected situation won't be a benefit in their minds." The mayor nodded at the ledger. "Please, take your time going through there. You may see something that I missed."

"You mentioned ledgers tracking crimes and punishment," Greer said. "Mind if we also look at those?"

"Sure, not a problem." The mayor went over to a worn and stained box. "They're all in here, as far as I can tell. Help yourself. If you don't mind, though, I'd like the ledgers to stay here. I'm trying to digitize this collection so that those who need these records can access them online." She straightened and looked at both Remi and Greer. "Understanding the past, this cult, everything that happened—it goes a long way toward healing."

Greer sent a look around the empty building. "That's

a big job. Are you doing it yourself?"

"I have help a few mornings a week. Gradually, the remaining residents are beginning to trust me. I was elected into office, but as I'm an apostate, it's still been an uphill slog. I think those who lived through the town's fall are seeing that some structure is better than the complete collapse that was well in progress before I took office—even for those with an extreme distrust of government."

"You're doing some great things here, mayor," Remi said. "You're brave to take this on."

Ester shrugged. "I don't know about brave, but I am determined. The people here have suffered enough. They deserve to move freely into the twenty-first century, unencumbered by their past. They're going to have to do that somewhere—I hope they can do it here." She nodded at a nearby table. "Why don't you get settled there? We have a water dispenser in the kitchen. I can put a pot of coffee on, if you like."

"The water will be fine. Thank you." Remi followed her into the kitchen to fetch the water while Greer brought the box of crime ledgers over to the table. Everyone settled around the table and began searching through them for clues to what happened with her mother.

After a while, Remi looked up from the old pages. "There's no mention of my mom's death or burial. Not in any page from thirteen years ago up to the last page. The last entry was about nine months ago."

"Are you sure your mom came back here?" the

mayor asked.

Remi nodded. "I know she made it back to this area. I have letters she sent." Remi pulled those out of a folder in her briefcase. The envelopes were postmarked from a nearby town.

"Okay." The mayor looked at the ledger pages in front of her. "When we spoke over the phone, you'd said you left about seventeen years ago. I see where the church seized your home once it declared you and your mother to be apostates." She gave Remi a worried look. "Do you want to read it?"

Remi nodded. Ester pushed the binder over to her. Remi stared at the words, smoothing her fingertips over the punishment that had been handed down. They meant different things to her and her mother. For her mom, leaving the Grummonds was an end of life as she knew it. She'd lost her community, her property—really, her value as a human. For Remi at the time, it meant the start of a new adventure in the scary world outside the small community that had been her home. There was danger, but excitement too.

"Two things," Greer said, interrupting her thoughts. "When your mom came back, she would have still been an outcast. She wouldn't have stayed on Grummond property."

"She stayed with a friend in the next town over. Her friend was also an apostate."

"So it probably doesn't make sense that we're looking for her grave in the Grummond cemetery."

"Except the letters I received were from active

members. If she had died while she was with her friend, her friend would have said that in her letter. She didn't. She just said that my mom came here one day and didn't return."

Greer nodded. "And the second thing... There are pages missing from this registry of punishments dating to that time period. Six months are missing." He showed Remi and the mayor the section that had missing pages. "It doesn't look like a recent tear. The torn edges are discolored and a little frayed."

Remi felt gut-punched. She leaned back in her seat. "We're never going to know what happened to her. Her friends are dead or have disappeared. The record is incomplete."

"Wait," Ester said. "She's here. It says she made restitution and has atoned for her crimes against the Society. She rejoined the Grummonds."

A chill went down Remi's neck. She looked at the mayor, then at Greer. "She hated them, hated everything they stood for. Why would she rejoin them?"

"The friend she stayed with outside of town might know. Have you tried looking for her?" the mayor asked.

"We have," Greer said. "Nothing popped in any system that I could find. I ran several queries based on her facial features, even aged her by seventeen years. Again, nada. She left the house she'd been renting shortly after her letter reporting Joan's death reached Remi."

Silence settled around the table for a long moment.

"I don't know where to go from here," the mayor said. "Were there any missing person reports filed on your mom's friend?"

"None that I could find," Greer said.

"You're both welcome to go over to the cemetery and have a look around. The graves age from front to back. They date back several decades, so if your mom was buried there but not recorded, she'd be somewhere in the last third of the graves. Of course, you're welcome to look through the whole cemetery. I was just trying to save you some time."

Remi closed the ledger. Her mind was still muddled by the fact that her mom had rejoined the Grummonds. As far as Remi knew, Mom was just coming back for a visit with her friends. There were several of them she'd secretly stayed in contact with. Remi always thought her mom's visit was only going to be a short-term thing.

Greer wrapped his warm hand around her cold one as he led her from the building. Outside, the world was the same as it had been before it had been shattered. Brilliant blue sky. Cold spring air. The sun was lower, pouring orange tones over the east side of the valley and blue shadows over the west side.

Greer walked her to the passenger door. "The letters you received all said she died of pneumonia. Was she sick when she left you?"

Remi nodded. "Not desperately ill, but she did have a late summer cold."

He opened her door. "Let's go see what we can find while we have daylight."

3

The drive to the cemetery was short. A tall wrought-iron fence surrounded the whole area. The front gate was an elaborate work of winged angels playing harps and cherubs with trumpets. Greer looked to see how Remi was reacting to this visit. On the plus side, the town had been open to their visit. On the minus side was the terrible new revelation that Remi's mom had rejoined the Grummonds. It was an inexplicable choice, and there was no one to ask why Joan had made it.

The cemetery itself was large. It housed hundreds of graves. They would run out of daylight if they went row by row. "Want to start in the middle?" Greer asked.

"Yeah. You start in the middle. I'll hit a few rows from the end, and we'll meet up."

"Sounds good." Greer didn't want to tell her that there were several dead people with them, some fully formed spirits, some just wisps of smoky fog. "So, um, what did your mom look like?"

Remi immediately knew they weren't alone. She sent a nervous glance around them. "Shit, Greer. Seriously?"

He nodded.

"She had shoulder-length brown hair, lighter than mine. She was about my height, slim."

"Got it."

As Remi moved several rows away, Greer shut his eyes and centered his energy. Keeping his senses open, as his grandfather had long ago taught him, Greer walked among the headstones, checking dates. There was something here, he felt certain. Whether it was Joan Chase was yet to be seen.

He looked over at Remi. She was moving quickly through her rows. She looked up, catching him watching her, and shook her head. "These are too new. How about you? Getting close to the time we're looking for?"

"I am." He resumed his stroll until he came to an elaborate headstone. Most of the others in the cemetery were simple, regular headstones. A few here and there were taller or more ornate. But this one had a marble angel standing behind it, his hands on the top of the headstone, its head bowed as if in mourning.

Esrom Stanton.

"Um, Remi? Come over here."

She cut through the rows separating them and stood beside him.

"He died the month your mom came back," Greer

said. "Just days after she was accepted back into the Society."

"I knew he'd died sometime around my mom's death, but didn't realize it was so close to hers." She closed her eyes and took a deep breath. "Wait a minute...you're not saying his death had something to do with my mom's, are you?"

"I'm just stating facts, at the moment." Remi shivered and folded her arms. He wrapped an arm around her shoulder. "Let's get this done. We only have a few more rows. I have a sneaking suspicion that your mom's not here."

"Yeah. And I'm hungry."

"We'll hit the diner after this. Tomorrow, we can spend more time with those ledgers."

They went through the remaining rows that had death dates around the time of her mom's visit. Neither her Society name nor the secular one she'd chosen was on any of the headstones.

They left the cemetery, feeling the weight of all of their unanswered questions. They didn't speak on the drive to the diner. Several cars were in the parking lot. Lights were on, warming the place. Inside, delicious scents filled the air. And though the decor looked left over from the nineties, no one inside seemed to mind its stale appearance.

A waitress came over. The woman was middle-aged. Her long hair was pinned up behind her head. She didn't look especially friendly. In fact, she looked wiped out. Her eyes were shadowed with gray circles.

"What can I get you to drink?" she asked.

They both ordered unsweetened iced teas. The woman had a pad of paper and a pen in her hand, but she didn't jot their order down—she just stared at Remi for an uncomfortably long moment.

When she left, Remi gave him a look that said more than words could. Another waitress stood in the hallway leading to the bathrooms. Greer caught her gaze. She stepped back into the hall. When he didn't take the summons, she looked at him again before again stepping back.

"I'm going to wash my hands," Greer said. "If the waitress comes by, order two cheeseburgers for me."

Remi nodded.

Greer went down the hallway. It was longer than he'd expected, but in addition to the restrooms, there was an office and a storeroom. The woman was standing at the back of the hall, draped in shadows. He wondered if the women's room was occupied. He nodded at her, then tried to ignore her as he set a hand on the door to the men's room.

"You're looking for Joan," the woman said, her voice barely a whisper.

Greer stopped, then slowly looked at her. "How did you know?"

"It's a small town."

"Did you know her?"

The woman nodded. "You aren't going to find her here."

"Do you know where she is?"

The woman took a napkin and pen out of her pocket. She pressed them up against the wall and started drawing. The road in front of the diner, leading to another road, leading to another. And then a footpath.

Jesus. Greer knew what she was laying out for him.

Graves, scattered out on the desert.

The woman added some land features. Rock outcroppings. Then she started to mark several different rectangles. On one, she drew an X.

Oh, fuck. He did not want to have to show this to Remi.

The woman looked over his shoulder as she handed him the map. He looked behind him in time to see another waitress step out of sight. When he looked back, the woman he'd been talking to was gone, and the door to the women's bathroom was closing.

"Wait. What's your name?" he asked into the narrowing opening. He needed to get her name in case he had to come back with questions.

"Coralee."

When Greer got back to the table, Remi was looking a little irritated.

"Haven't seen the waitress." She laughed. "Sorry to be so grouchy. I think I'm hangry."

Greer took a ten-dollar bill out of his wallet and dropped it on the table to pay for the drinks and service they didn't receive. "We can't stay anyway. I have some protein bars in the SUV." He rushed Remi out of the diner and to their car.

He dug a couple of his snacks out and handed them to Remi.

"Want to tell me what happened in there?" she asked.

He pulled out of the parking lot and headed down the road, the first of the three the waitress had drawn for him. "I got a lead on where your mom's body might be."

Remi straightened and turned to face him. "Where?"

"A little ways out of town. I want to get out there before we lose daylight."

"There must be another cemetery." She looked at the road they were moving down. "It wouldn't surprise me at all to find the Grummonds segregated their members into true followers who were placed in the cemetery for the elites and one for those members who were less-than-stellar followers or who were merely commoners in the Grummond hierarchy."

"It's sad to think the group would judge its members so harshly."

"Fear of the afterlife is a powerful tool. Did you know that some religious cults like the Grummonds require their wives to keep their hair long so that they can bathe their husband's feet in the afterlife?"

Greer looked at her, then at her thick brown locks, then grinned.

"Don't even think about it," she warned him.

He laughed as he turned onto the next road that had been on that map. They drove out of town long enough for the dusky sky to noticeably darken. He was supposed to have taken the first right, but having gone almost ten miles, he'd begun to think he'd missed the turn. Just then, a narrow dirt road broke through the sage and rabbit brush. He turned toward it, his lights illuminating the rough path. At least it was a path—the only one he'd noticed in the long drive out.

"I don't think this is right," Remi said. "It's too far from town."

Greer didn't say anything. It was a great spot for an ambush. He drove as far down the road as he could, then parked. "Stay in the car. If there's anything to see, I'll come get you."

Remi looked worried. He knew she'd been through enough, because of the Grummonds, to know she needed to follow his advice. "Be careful."

He nodded once. He went to the back hatch and opened the weapons stash. He took out his M9 and slipped it into his holster. He strapped a KA-BAR to his thigh. "Lock up after me." He grabbed a steel flashlight and shut the hatch, then walked into the biting wind. At least the cold meant he wouldn't have to watch for rattlers as he moved through the unfamiliar territory.

The girl had drawn some of the land features on her map: the canyon walls, large rock outcroppings, the draws that led down to the dry ravine. It looked like he was in the right place…but the right place for what?

There were no human tracks in the pinkish, powdery dirt. No one had been out here in a long time—if ever. He turned around and shined his light in a broad sweep around this side of the ridge. No cars. No buildings.

Nothing but rabbit brush, sage, yucca, dried weeds, and stunted scrub pines. And wind. Lots and lots of wind.

The light of the setting sun gave the distant rim of the canyon an iridescent purple glow. He went over the rise in front of him and came to a hard stop.

Aw, hell. This was bad.

Dozens, maybe hundreds of graves stretched across the vista, some marked, some sunken into the ground. Some human remains were visible and scattered about. Greer wondered if their corpses had been disturbed by animals. Maybe they'd never even been buried.

Jesus. To think Remi's mom was dumped out here, forgotten.

Greer looked at his phone. No bars. He needed to get a hold of Owen. This whole area might be a crime scene. Greer dreaded having to show the site to Remi, but he couldn't keep it from her.

He walked back to the SUV. She rolled down the window as he approached. They exchanged a long look.

"You need to come see," he said at last.

Remi shut her eyes. Greer knew she was drawing strength to face what he'd found. She rolled the window back up and got out while he shut the SUV off and locked it. She followed him up the slight ridge.

"Oh, God," she whispered. "No." She covered her mouth as she looked around in horror at the graves his flashlight revealed. "You think my mom's here?"

"The lady who sent us here believed she was."

"That would explain why she wasn't in the Grummond registry. Why would they do this?"

Greer shook his head. "Why would they have done anything they did? Force children to marry. Force women to be one of many wives. Force religion—a twisted version at that—on their members. Force members to exist outside of mainstream society. I don't know. I do think this feels like a punishment of some sort."

"Can we look around?"

"I guess. Let's not disturb anything."

A couple of the graves had rough crosses made from sticks and twine. Some had names carved on them; some didn't. Some had no crosses at all.

"How are we going to find her?" Remi asked.

Greer remembered the drawing he'd been given. The waitress had marked a certain grave. He reached into his pocket for the napkin she'd drawn on, but it wasn't there. He checked his other pockets, but couldn't find it. He looked back on the trail, wondering if it had fallen out. No matter. He remembered the drawing perfectly.

"The waitress back at the diner felt certain your mom's grave was near a certain outcropping—one with three points."

Remi took his flashlight and swept it over the sprawling landscape. "There." She held the light on an outcropping that fit the description.

Greer followed her over that way. There was a grave next to the rocks. It was one of the few with a cross, but the sticks were grayed and brittle. The light caught a shimmer of something. Remi started forward, but Greer stopped her. "I'll get it."

He knelt near the cross. A thin gold chain with a tiny locket hung there. He took it off the cross, then stepped back to give it to Remi. She gasped. Her eyes filled with tears as she looked at what she held.

"It was Mom's. She always wore it."

Greer held the light on the necklace as Remi opened the locket. More than a decade of weathering had roughened the casing, but the two pictures inside were still intact. One of little Remi. One of her mom.

Remi started crying. Greer pulled her close. "I'm sorry, babe. This isn't the closure I'd hoped to give you. We'll have to report this to the authorities. At best, it's an unsanctioned graveyard. At worst, it's a crime scene. And we'll need to confirm that this grave is your mom's."

She nodded against his chest. Sniffling, she stepped back.

He moved a heavy lock of her hair behind her ear. "I'm going to set a GPS pin so we can get back here tomorrow." He marked where they were standing.

"Do you think the mayor knows about this place?"

"We can ask her in the morning. I need to call Owen so he can call in a forensic team. Let's get back to town. I had cell service there."

Remi was quiet on the long drive back. Greer didn't try to get her to talk. He was hoping a hot meal at the diner would help her reset, but when they pulled into the parking lot, it was empty, and the diner appeared to be closed. No, not empty...long abandoned was more like it.

He and Remi exchanged confused glances. He got

out to look in through the cloudy glass door. He pulled on the door, surprised it wasn't locked, but then, very few people lived in town anymore. And even fewer visitors came through. Anything of value was probably long ago picked through. He went inside. A thick layer of dust covered every surface. The only chairs that were upright were the ones he and Remi had used earlier. His ten-dollar bill was still on the table.

Shit.

They would have been waiting forever for their order.

He went back outside. In the headlights, he waved his ten-dollar bill at Remi. When he got back inside the SUV, she said, "I hate your ghosts, Greer. I really do."

"I get that. But my ghosts helped us find your mom, so…" He took out his phone and called Owen.

"You find Remi's mom?" Owen asked, bypassing pleasantries.

"I think so, but not where we expected her to be. We found what looks like an undocumented graveyard with hundreds of graves. One grave had her necklace on a wooden cross. It may or may not be her."

"Right. I'll call it in. You going to be there tomorrow?"

"We will be. We're spending the night in a local B&B. We'll be taking the mayor out to the site sometime tomorrow."

"Copy that. I'll text you any updates."

"Thanks, Owen."

"Yeah. Tell Remi I'm sorry it went this way. You had a gut feel something was off."

"I did, and I will."

Greer hung up and looked at Remi, who'd been listening. She reached for his hand.

"You still feel like staying at the B&B here in town?" Greer asked.

She nodded. "I want to be here until they find my mom."

"We may not have that info right away. It'll take time to do the forensics."

"Can we at least stay until we know the bodies are being moved into the proper custody?"

Greer nodded. "We can stay a few days."

"I don't want to lose track of my mom again."

Greer kissed her knuckles. "We'll make it work."

4

R emi's shock had deepened by the time they got back to the B&B. Greer was worried Abel would have shut the place down for the night, but it wasn't as late as he feared.

"Not a word about what we found, at least not until we know more about him. I sent his info over to Max to get a profile on him," Greer warned Remi, seconds before their host came to greet them.

"Did you have a good—" Abel looked at Remi. "I was going to ask if you'd had a nice visit so far, but I can tell you haven't. Are you hungry? I typically only offer breakfast with your room, but I know there aren't many food options in town…yet. I'm trying to talk a friend into reopening the diner."

He moved deeper into the house, heading for the kitchen. He was full of cheerful chatter, which made the horrific evening feel a little more normal.

"The trust took everything they could liquidate when

new members were forced onto the board by the state after the town's collapse. The trust was late in its property tax payments. They gutted the diner and sold off what property they could," Abel said as he opened his fridge and took out sandwich fixings. He looked at Remi, then at Greer, obviously concerned about Remi's mood.

"What brings you here to Blanco Ridge?" he asked.

"We came to retrieve Remi's mom's body. We live up by Laramie, so we wanted her closer to us."

"That's good idea. Did you find her?"

Greer shook his head. "Not in town. That's the problem."

"Ah." Abel stared at the countertop a long moment. "The hell of it all, as if the Grummonds didn't take enough from all of us—they steal our dead, too." He looked at Remi. "I'm sorry. You're welcome to stay here as long as you like. I don't exactly have customers beating down the doors yet."

"Thank you," Remi said.

WHEN THEY FINISHED with their meal, Greer ushered Remi up to their room. She looked like she was falling asleep on her feet. He started a shower for her, then brought her pajamas in so she wouldn't catch a chill afterward.

A little while later, when they were both in bed, lying close, he kissed her forehead. He loved the way she curled into him. "Don't think about it tonight. Don't think about anything."

"I can't shut off my mind."

"We don't want to get ahead of ourselves. Owen is sending the right experts down. They'll be able to determine exactly what we're dealing with. And since so many of the Grummonds' upper tier are in custody and awaiting trials, this will get prompt attention."

"I don't want it bungled. I don't want my mom's remains mixed with someone else's."

"Right. Tomorrow, or whenever they begin exhumations, we'll make sure the remains pulled from the grave that had her necklace on it are properly labeled. But we can't take custody of them until they give her a cause of death—and they determine she's your mom."

"You think her death wasn't from natural causes?"

"With the Grummonds—or the Omnis or the WKB —I don't believe anything they might say." He didn't want to tell her that he had questions around the fact that Esrom Stanton died shortly after Joan returned to the Society. She'd been nursing a vendetta ever since Remi had been selected to marry Senator Whiddon.

Maybe Greer was just superimposing his own behavior onto Remi's mom.

Maybe Joan really had wanted to return to the group that had been her family for so many years.

Maybe those answers would never be fully known.

THE NEXT MORNING dawned clear and cold. Abel puttered about. Greer sensed he was hoping to be asked to sit and chat with them as they ate the omelets he'd made them. He and Remi exchanged a look, then Remi said, "This is the best omelet I've ever had, Abel."

Word had come back from Max that Abel was exactly as he portrayed himself to be in his bio on the B&B's website—a former Grummond Society member turned apostate turned innkeeper.

Greer lifted the insulated coffee pitcher and gestured toward their innkeeper. "Bring your cup over here and join us—if you can take a break."

"I can." Abel grabbed a fresh mug from a stack of them and came over. He pulled a chair out and sat at their table. "Sorry. If I'm intruding, tell me. I'm still new at this B&B stuff. All the forums and guidebooks say to leave guests alone, but I'm starving for human conversation."

"I can understand that," Greer said.

"Business has been slow going so far, but I've only been open since the first of the year. Mayor Sullivan and her team are trying to figure out how to reinvent the town. I hope they're successful. We're surrounded by beautiful countryside here. That alone is worth the visit. Great fishing and hunting. Great hikes. It's an awesome place to unplug. It's also a dead zone."

Remi looked at Greer, then frowned at Abel. "What do you mean by that?" she asked.

Abel shook his head and held up his hands. "It's like

a curse is hanging over this place. Like the trauma of all that happened here has left its shadow."

"A friend of mine knows a shaman who clears stuff like that out," Greer said. "I know he clears homes; maybe he could clear a town."

"Maybe he could, but until the disease that's still here is eradicated, not sure it would be of much use."

"Disease?" Remi asked.

"The town's broken. The government's repossessed most of the community's properties for overdue taxes. They've seized the assets of the people and businesses that historically paid those taxes, so there's no money to pay them anyway. Decades ago, the Society elders put all of the church property into a trust so that they could have control of who got what benefits. The regular members were hoodwinked into believing that turning over their property to the church was, in effect, handing it over to God to manage. So long as they complied with every expectation the Society had of them, they were rewarded with jobs, housing, wives. When things got so bad after the Prophet Josiah died, the trust was handed to a state judge for oversight. New members were put on the board, turning it into a secular management group. It has good intentions of getting citizens into or back into their own houses, but the people here have significant distrust of all governmental activities. And some even think that anything the government has ever touched has violated the sanctity of the trust's original purpose. It's a tangled mess. People are squatting in shanties they put out on the fringes of town while their homes in town slowly fall apart. We need to get them back into their houses. Get their places repaired and the utilities turned back on. Find jobs for them. Get the town functioning again." He stopped and stared into his coffee cup. "I'm sorry. I don't mean to ramble so."

"I know some of what you're going through. I was born here," Remi said. "Lived here until I was fourteen. I was a child bride of Prophet Josiah."

"Shit," Abel said, shaking his head. "I'm glad you got out."

"Me too. But my mom came back and died shortly after her return."

"Ah. That explains a lot. Sorry that happened."

"Thanks. Coming back here, it all seems so fresh and raw."

"I was a member of the Grummonds most of my life. I left when the woman I loved was forced to marry her cousin."

"Oh, God," Remi whispered.

"What happened to her?" Greer asked.

"I talked her into leaving with me, but she couldn't adjust to life as an apostate," Abel replied. "She came back to the Society and married that son of a bitch. She had a kid with him. They're some of those living in the shanties, trying to eke out a living. They're why I came back. She still won't talk to me, but I'm working on breaking through." He smiled. "She's worth fighting for." He sipped his coffee. "So what's your plan for today?"

Remi drew a harsh breath. "I think we found my

mom. Did you know there's another graveyard outside of town?"

Abel shut his eyes and nodded. "Is that where your mom is?"

"I think so. It's bad out there. A team is coming in to check it out. The mayor had no burial records for my mom."

"Do you think Ester knew about that cemetery?" Greer asked.

Abel nodded. "Everyone here did. The adults, at least. It was one of the things the leaders used to threaten us with. So much of the Grummond philosophy was tied up in the belief in the paradise of our afterlife. They made it clear that infractions against the Society would land someone in that unconsecrated boneyard, which would keep them from that promised paradise. A lot of people ended up there. Some people ended there, if you know what I mean."

"They were taken there and murdered?" Greer asked.

"Yup. It was an effective deterrent, especially after Father Esrom died. The Prophet Josiah wasn't a full-time resident here. The lieutenants he put in charge went power-crazy...and they made good use of that hell-hole. That's part of the disease that still keeps this place in its grip. I'm glad you've alerted the authorities about it. That's one cancer that could be healed."

Greer's phone buzzed as a text came in. Owen wrote that Montezuma County was sending a deputy sheriff and its coroner to the site midmorning. Greer told Remi.

"Hey—want a third wheel to tag along?" Abel asked. "I could pack us a lunch. Things are quiet here."

Remi and Greer exchanged looks. Remi gave a quick nod, then Greer said, "Works for us. I updated the mayor a little bit ago. When you're ready, we'll go pick her up, then head out to the site."

"Great! I'll add a sandwich for her."

Mayor Sullivan was standing outside waiting for them when they parked next to the small town hall building. "Morning."

Remi nodded, finding it a little difficult not to get emotional all over again.

"Greer says you may have found your mom," the mayor said.

"I hope so," Remi said, "but it's heartbreaking to find out where she was. Now we want to know what happened to her…and all the others out there."

"Thanks for picking me up. A discovery like this is something a mayor should have a handle on, I think."

"Did you know about that cemetery?" Greer asked.

The mayor pursed her lips. "We'd all heard rumors about it. None of us was really brave enough to go looking for it. At least, no one I know of. Even asking about it made people disappear from the Society. It was something I was going to suggest to you, but I didn't know where it was, if it was real, or if it was safe to investigate."

The ride out to the gravesite didn't seem to take as long this time as it had last night. A couple of vehicles joined them on the long dirt road—too far back to make out details, like the presence of emergency vehicle lighting. Greer hoped they were the county officials coming out to meet them. He looked in the rearview mirror. If they weren't, he had three civilians he had to keep safe.

A few minutes later, two white SUVs parked next to him at the site—one was the sheriff's, and the other had a county coroner emblem on the front door.

Still, he didn't want to take any chances. "Hang tight a minute."

He got out and greeted the team of three men and a woman—two were deputy sheriffs, the woman was the coroner, and the third man was her assistant. Greer waved at his SUV, inviting his passengers out to join the group. He made all the introductions.

"Why don't you tell us what we're going to be looking at?" Dr. Morgan Wallis, the county coroner, said.

"It's an unconsecrated gravesite used by the Grummond Society, probably for decades," Ester said.

The deputy sheriff gave the mayor a critical look. "How long have you known about this place?"

"I've known about it—in theory—all my life, but never knew it actually existed. It was held over the Society members' heads like a boogieman—anyone who broke the rules was threatened with ending up here. People who talked about it or tried to find it often ended up disappearing."

Greer could see that Remi's hackles were rising at what it seemed the deputy was implying. "Mayor Sullivan has inherited a deeply rooted mess," Remi said. "She's trying to clean it up as each new challenge is presented."

"Uh-huh. And how are you involved in this?" the deputy asked.

"I believe my mom's buried here."

"And what makes you believe that?"

"We were told we'd find her body here," Greer said.

"Who told you that?" the deputy asked.

"A woman in town."

The deputy took out a small pad of paper and a pen. "Why don't you give me her name? I'm going to want to interview her."

"That's going to be hard to do," Greer said.

"Why?"

"Because she's dead."

The deputy looked shocked. "When did that happen?"

"Who knows? She was a ghost when I spoke to her."

The deputy's body language shifted as he looked at Greer in disbelief. "You rounded all of us up on a priority call-out for shits and giggles?" He got up in Greer's face. "I don't think you'll be laughing when you get the bill for making a false police report."

"Deputy, with all due respect," Greer said, "why don't we go have a look at the site before you send me that bill?"

"Agreed," the coroner said. She draped her camera's wide strap around her neck.

Greer noticed the mayor was frowning at the deputy. "I recognize you," Ester said. "You were a member of the Society. You were on the God squad."

"I was a member of the Grummonds' security forces, yes."

"So did you know about this graveyard?" Ester asked.

The deputy's face hardened, a clear tell. "Like you, I'd heard rumors."

Greer supposed he shouldn't be surprised that a former Grummond would have stayed in the area, finding work where he could. He didn't like the guy's attitude or the facile way he'd almost implicated the mayor.

"It's just over that hill," Greer said, leading the group.

When they crested the low ridge, he heard their collective gasps. In the daylight, it was easy to see the dozens of rustic stick crosses sticking up. There was no order to the arrangement of graves—it looked like they were scattered over a couple of acres. What was more shocking than the graves were the clumps of exposed bones.

"I knew this was real," the coroner said in a hushed voice. "A few years back, a local teen brought us footage from his drone as it flew over this area. The quality of the video was pretty poor, but we could make out the graves. His drone was shot down." She looked at the mayor. "When we asked your predecessor for permission to look into the report, we were denied. I'm glad you brought this forward. I'll be taking custody of this site, deputy. We'll establish a perimeter this morning. I could use a couple of your officers assigned to us for the next week or so."

The deputy pursed his mouth, then nodded. "I'll call it in."

"Mayor, is there a warehouse or large hall in town where we could setup a command post?" the coroner asked.

"Yes," Ester said. "We have an old meetinghouse that hasn't been used in months. I'll get it ready for you. Do you need anything else? Additional staff, supplies?"

"I'll let you know."

"Dr. Wallis," Remi said, "I believe that grave over by that outcropping belongs to my mother. I can't... I don't want to lose her again."

The coroner nodded. "Every one of these graves is someone's loved one. We'll take care with her remains and all of those here."

5

The coroner and her team settled into the Prophet's B&B. Their work was going to take every bit of the next two weeks. They wanted to move quickly before the spring storms came in. With the graves in varying states of disinterment, a heavy spring storm would wreak further havoc on the site, so she had teams of forensic investigators working in two shifts. Students from several universities came in to help. The coroner ran the operation with the efficiency of an army sergeant, organizing the chaos into a forward marching machine.

Greer and Remi had spent the week in town. Remi couldn't miss more time from her classes at the university.

Greer slipped his arms around her, drawing her back against him. They were standing in the Grummonds' abandoned brick meetinghouse, looking at the dozens of forensic experts working on several dozen bodies excavated from their shallow graves. Floor lights were set up over every steel table. The examiners wore hair caps and nitrile gloves. White coats were buttoned over their street clothes. The operation wasn't as sterile as a computer clean room, but it was damned close.

Off to one end, there was a small lunch area set up that several of the women in town were running. Coffee was kept hot and water kept cold, and sandwiches were constantly being restocked in a large cooler.

"Look at this, Remi. What do you see?" Greer asked.

"I see hell come to life. So many bodies dumped as if they didn't matter."

Greer reached in front of her and lifted off a pretend baseball cap, replacing it with another invisible one. "Take off your daughter's hat and put on your sociologist's hat. Now what do you see?"

She stared at the room in silence, resisting his suggestion. "I can't. I'm too close."

"I see a town healing by acknowledging its turbulent and criminal history. I see true followers of the Society standing next to apostates and outsiders. I see a town that has shunned any government interference welcoming its experts so that the town can better understand what happened in its past. This is huge, Remi. Huge. And you did this."

"How did I do this?"

"You persisted in your search for your mother's remains. You threw the door open and let everyone come in or leave as they wanted."

Remi shook her head. "I didn't do that. The town

did. The town was finally ready to move beyond what it was to become what it could be."

"Yes, but you were the tipping point."

Remi wrapped her arms over his at her waist. "I just want my mom, Greer."

"We'll have her soon. I think she's very proud you."

Remi's eyes were swimming with tears as she looked up at him. "You think so?" She straightened as a thought occurred to her. "Do you see her here?"

Greer's smile was a little sad. "No. But what mother wouldn't be proud of a daughter like you?"

She bowed her head against his chest and wrapped her arms around him. "I love you."

Her words filled him with joy. "That makes me the happiest man alive. I love you too."

She blinked her tears away. "Let's head back to the B&B, see if Abel needs help for the herd of people coming in at the end of the day."

AFTER DINNER THAT NIGHT, Greer and Remi sat at the kitchen table with Abel and the mayor.

"I'm sorry you'll be leaving tomorrow," Ester said. "Since the election, I've been moving forward so carefully, taking baby steps so I wouldn't alienate anyone more than necessary. You guys came in like a whirlwind and blew everything wide open. I wouldn't have thought to do that, but turns out, it worked."

"What's next for the town?" Greer asked.

Ester looked at Abel. "There's so much to be done," she said. "We need to get families out of those steel shanties and back into houses. There are plenty held by the church trust, but it won't turn them over without the new owners taking classes to better understand what's expected of them in their civic responsibilities so that they can manage their real estate holdings without losing them to unpaid taxes. And the trust won't grant them loans to cover those things without their having an income source."

"So, jobs," Greer said.

"Jobs. Housing. Education. Healthcare. Food. All of it." Ester sighed. "We're starting from scratch."

"The town has rich possibilities," Abel said. "We're surrounded by Pueblo and Anasazi ruins. We're close to the Four Corners area. We have a large hot spring on trust property. And that's not even including all the hiking, camping, horseback riding, ATV paths in the area—we could make this a big tourist destination for outdoorsy types."

"But we need the infrastructure to support tourism," Ester said. "Beyond this B&B, we don't have hotels, restaurants, or grocery stores. Nor do we have the workforce or systems in place to manage our natural resources."

"You can't get it all done at once," Greer said. "Take some small steps. There are more houses here than families who need them. Maybe you could open rentals for tourists. And there are plenty of people needing the work, which they could do with a little training."

Remi leaned her elbows on the table as she smiled at Ester. "Several of the colleges and universities in Colorado feature urban planning programs. You might consider reaching out to them to see if there's any opportunity to partner with them as you rebuild the town."

Ester stared at Remi as she processed that suggestion. "I would love the guidance. I left the Society ten years ago, but because I wasn't brought up in the secular world, I'm missing so much of the governance models I need, which I feel awful about. I'm the mayor. I'm supposed to lead our town through this transition."

"I think you're doing a great job," Greer said.

"Several of my friends have skill sets that might be of use to you," Remi said. "And while I can't volunteer them, I'm happy to ask if they'd be willing to at least chat with you, maybe consult as needed. Ivy runs a diner where we live. She could talk to you about getting your diner reopened."

"I know the perfect person to run it," Abel said, giving the mayor a sheepish grin. "The lady I'm thinking of is an amazing cook. And everyone in town loves her."

"Unfortunately, being sweet and talented doesn't provide the startup capital a business like that would need," the mayor said. "Nor does she have the experience that she would need to keep a business afloat."

"But there are grants available," Remi replied. "And there are angel investors. There are training programs. And a proper business plan might persuade the trustees to open their purse strings."

"Our friend Blade is a financial savant," Greer said.

"He might be willing to consult with the trustees on investments that would grow their holdings so they could do more for the residents here."

"And several of our friends live in an off-grid community where they grow or trade for everything they need," Remi said. "They might be able to help you discover some self-sufficiency options. They're rebuilding their community too."

"Were they a polygamist society too?" Ester asked.

Greer shook his head. "No. But their isolationist philosophy set them up for manipulation from some of the same bad actors who partnered with the Grummond leadership. They have a fair amount in common with you guys."

Greer could see that the wheels were starting to turn in Ester's mind. She looked at Abel. "We might have a shot at this."

"We *do* have a shot at it," he said, laughing.

GREER GRINNED at Remi as they entered their room. She narrowed her eyes at him. "What?"

"Nothing. I'm just happy."

She smiled as she slipped into his arms. "What are you happy about?"

"Everything. You. This town. The fact that we found your mom and will have her near us soon. I'm happy Coralee gets the closure she needed."

Remi stepped back. "Did you say Coralee?"

"Yup."

"How do you know her?"

"I don't. But she expended a huge amount of energy to get info of your mom's grave to us."

Remi was still frowning.

"She was the ghost that drew the map for me in the diner."

"Oh my God. My mom stayed with her when she came back here. Coralee was her Society name. She never used it after she left. There's no way you could have known her by that name." She gave Greer a sad look. "I guess her reaching out to you means she's also dead."

Greer nodded. "Geez. That was a rough way to break that news. I'm sorry."

Remi shook her head. "You didn't know. And I shouldn't be surprised. At least now we know not to search for her. Do you think she was also in the graveyard?"

Greer nodded. "Maybe. Being a friend of your mom's, she was probably a dissident as well." He set his hands on Remi's shoulders and started to gently massage the tension knotting her muscles. After a minute, she groaned and leaned into his chest. He continued to work the tension from her neck, then used both hands on her back, kneading the muscles above her shoulder blades, then between them. He was happy to give her ease for as long as she let him.

Each time she started to withdraw, he'd say, "Not yet. There's a knot here too." Fifteen minutes in, she was completely limp. He picked her up, then carried her to their bed.

She moaned as she stretched out. Greer began to unbutton her blouse. She set her hands on his, stopping him. "We can't have sex here. I can't do it in a place like this, with the history it has."

"We're not having sex." He kissed her neck, the soft front part of her throat.

"It feels as if we are."

"Nope. I'm checking you for tension."

"With your lips?"

"Lips are very sensitive."

Remi shut her eyes and nodded. "Yes. Well, continue, then. I feel tense all over."

Greer grinned against her skin, using kisses to distract her from the buttons he was freeing. When her shirt was open, he helped her remove it. He yanked his tee off, then moved on top of her, pushing his hands beneath her shoulders to cup her neck and head, using a thumb to tilt her chin up so he could kiss the soft skin there.

"Greer, my bra is still on."

He lifted himself enough that he could pop the front clasp open, exposing her breasts. He trailed his fingers down the lush side of one breast, the stroke so feather-soft that it was barely there. Remi's eyes were closed, but Greer could tell how his touch affected her by the way she pushed against his fingers. Greer didn't let her take over their interaction; the more she pushed against him, the lighter his strokes became. He knew she caught on when she flattened her back and opened her eyes, watching him.

He smiled at her, his eyes hooded. Slowly, slowly, he bent close to kiss the underside of one breast. Remi hissed when his mouth made contact. "This isn't very relaxing, Greer."

He moved to the other breast. "These things take time."

"My jeans are still on."

Greer kissed her ribs. "Do you want them off?"

"Yes."

"Good." He unbuttoned her jeans and loosened the short zipper. Moving his knees outside her legs, he tugged the waist of her pants down, leaving her panties in place. She lifted her hips for him. He pulled the tight-fitting legs down until she could kick them off.

Kneeling over her, he pressed his face into her soft belly, rubbing his bristly jaw this way and that against her tender skin. When he looked up at her, she was bracing herself on her elbows, watching him. He smiled, glad she was entirely focused on him and not the man who used to live in this house—or the many, many girls who'd encountered abuse here.

He leaned over and nipped the edge of her hip.

She sucked in a sharp breath.

He dipped his tongue into her navel. Her lips went dry. He watched as she licked them. He couldn't help but think of her warm, moist mouth sucking his cock, nibbling along its sensitive underside. Remi must have been thinking the same thing, because her green eyes went dark, like shadows over a summer forest.

Greer pulled his attention from her eyes, closing his as he kissed the soft area between her bellybutton and her mound. He lifted one of her legs and dragged his teeth down her inner thigh.

Yeah, he could eat this woman alive. He was glad she was his, because he intended to do just that.

He repeated the stroke of his teeth against her other inner thigh, then dragged her thin panties down. Then, without warning or preamble, he scooped her up and flipped her over to finish pulling them off. He positioned her hands above her body and spent long minutes massaging her upper arms, her shoulders, her neck.

He moved down to her back, running his thumbs up the sides of her spine, from the top of her hips to the base of her skull. He massaged her hips, did deep-tissue work on her rounded ass cheeks. He spread her legs wider, then slipped two fingers between, finding her soft, wet folds and entering her. He felt her tighten around him and almost had an end event in his jeans.

When she started to push up, he put a hand on her shoulders and said, "Not yet."

She folded her arms under her head and rested her forehead on them. All the tension he'd just spent long minutes releasing throughout her body was back, but it was different this time. Now it was hot, liquid desire pulsing through her bones and muscles—pure, throbbing anticipation.

She was wet. Deliciously so. His fingers slipped in

and out. When he knew she was close to coming, he lifted her hips and, freeing himself, pushed into her, replacing his fingers with his cock. It only took a couple of strokes before her first orgasm hit. He grinned, knowing he was going to have to hold out for at another one or two before he'd give her body what it craved: his release.

He reached in front of her to stroke her clit. That was all it took to send her over the edge again.

At last it was his turn. He leaned over her raised hips. Bracing himself on his fists, he pumped into her, thrusting fast, feeling the pulsing hunger in his own cock. For a moment, he pressed his face into her back, then he straightened and grabbed her hips, holding her against himself as his release neared. He groaned his relief when his body let go.

They both collapsed on the bed, facing each other. Remi's expression was a mix of shadows and light. He stroked her cheek, waiting for her to speak first.

"We weren't supposed to have sex here," she whispered.

Greer smiled. "We didn't. We made love. Night and day difference."

Remi wrapped her arms around his neck and buried her face. "I wish you'd been here in those days."

"I do too. Whiddon wouldn't have been a problem for you. You would have been free to pick whoever you wanted."

Greer felt Remi's warm lips on his jaw. "I would have picked you."

"You sure about that?" He grinned. "I seem to remember you telling me you would have been babysitting me back in the day."

"Babysitting an assassin is just ridiculous."

"Yeah." He leaned over her until she was on her back. "I love you. I'm proud of you. We'll have your mom up near us before you know it."

She put her palm on his cheek as she stared into his eyes. "I love you too."

6

A month later, on the eve of his family's visit, Greer couldn't fall asleep. He wasn't worried, exactly, but it seemed a big change was coming.

Remi was sleeping peacefully. After all the trauma of their discovery weeks ago, and the tension of waiting for the results from the investigation into what had happened to her mom and all the others from the Grummond's boneyard, she was emotionally exhausted. He wanted to talk to her, but didn't want to disturb her.

He listened to her restful breathing for another hour before deciding to head downstairs so he wouldn't wake her. Most of the lights in the house were in night mode, so the lamp that was on in the living room seemed especially bright. Val was in one of the armchairs, reading.

"Want a nightcap?" Greer asked.

Val held up his whiskey glass. "Already had one."

"Want another?"

"Sure." He handed it to Greer. "What's got you up so late?"

"Thinking. My parents, sisters, and their families are all coming in tomorrow."

"I know."

Greer handed him his glass with fresh ice and a shot of Balcones. "I need help."

"Name it."

Greer sat on the ottoman in front of Val's armchair. "I need Ace to accept she's part of our family. How do we do that?"

Val sucked in a deep breath. He sipped his drink, then put his book down. "I don't know."

"I don't either. I mean, we'll include her in everything we do, but inclusion won't in itself make a determined outsider feel like an insider."

"Isolation has given Ace strength and insulated her from the worst of life for a long time," Val said.

"Yes. But now it might keep her from the best of life. I know my mom and dad are going to want some quality time with her while they're here. I don't have the heart to tell them not to try."

"If she allows that."

Greer nodded.

They sat in silence for a long moment.

"Let's talk to Rocco's counselor," Val said. "He might have some good suggestions."

"I'll call when they open tomorrow and see if he can spare an hour for us."

REMI LOOKED at her friends as they sat in the leather sofas in the billiards room. Greer and Max had gone down to Cheyenne to pick his family up. With the five kids his sisters had and the six adults, they'd needed two vehicles. Waiting for them gave her time to mentally prepare for the upcoming visit, something it seemed Ace was also doing.

"What are you most looking forward to about this visit, Ace?" Remi asked.

Like Greer, his sister had such unusual eye color. His were a light whiskey color. Ace's were a pale lichen green. Remi wondered if their other two sisters had as unusual an eye color as these two siblings.

"I've learned a lot about being in a family from my time here at Blade's," Ace said. "I thought I didn't need that, but I'm beginning to think I do. So I guess I'm looking forward to having a real visit with Greer's parents and getting to know his sisters. How about you?"

That answer made Remi happy.

"I had a big family when I was young. Growing up in the Grummond Society, I was surrounded by dozens of half-siblings and cousins. There was always someone to play with. I left that behind when I became a teenager. As a kid, I never gave much thought to what my mom was going through, being one of several wives, and a lesser one at that. After we left the cult, it was just the two of us for a long time. Since her death, I've sort of been adrift. Like you, I didn't think I needed or wanted the trouble or drama of a family. But now, being with Greer, seeing all of you together, I think I'm ready to be part of something bigger than myself. So really, I'm looking forward to all of it—meeting your sisters, their husbands, your parents, the kids, the chaos and emotion of it all. It would be nice to just belong somewhere."

"You belong with us," Val said.

"Thank you." Remi smiled. "It's funny. I've built a career around understanding human communities—healing toxic ones, rebuilding fractured ones, sustaining healthy ones—and yet I never felt as if I belonged to any community myself."

"You're a natural watcher," Val said. "Not like the pride watchers. Not a guard dog. You're an observer of human nature. It's almost impossible to clearly observe something you're part of, so it makes sense that you stay on the outside. It goes with the territory. But just because you feel like an outsider doesn't mean you are."

Ace nodded. "You're one of us because we claim you." She grinned. "You're our Spock from the *Enterprise* crew. Separate, but of us. Relentlessly analytical, but a wonderful component of the team."

Remi laughed. "So I'm an alien?"

"Yeah, but then again," Ace said, "in most situations, so were the entire *Enterprise* crew. So it works."

"You know," Remi said, "I'll take that."

A short while later, Ace and Val's phones buzzed.

They sent Remi a nervous look. "They're coming into town," Ace said.

Remi jumped off the sofa. "Oh, God." She flapped her hands. How crazy was it that she had no problem holding classes in a crowded lecture hall or presenting her research at conferences in front of critical peers, but meeting Greer's family tied knots in her gut?

Ace nodded. "Yeah."

"Okay." Remi straightened her shirt. "Well, their rooms are ready. Your sister—"

"Greer's sister," Ace interjected.

Remi shook her head, too distracted to deal with Ace's redirection. "Nancy's kids are from her husband's first marriage. His wife died a while ago. They're thirteen, eleven, and nine. When the girls heard about the basement bunkroom, they wanted to stay down there, and their brother, Billy, does everything they do. And then Tina and Steve's two young ones will stay with them."

Remi wrung her hands together, mentally going through all the arrangements, all of which had been shifting over the last two days. She and Greer had even considered setting the parents up in the classrooms downstairs, since they weren't in use now that the kids were in public school.

Ace laughed as she left the sofa and went over to still Remi's hands. "It's all good. We can move people around as we need to. I'm not worried about it."

Remi went still and stared at Ace. "I want them to like us."

58

"I don't give a fuck about them."

"You do too."

Ace shrugged. "We'll get through this. And I hope we'll have fun. We'll do our best; the rest is on them."

Remi nodded. "Right. Right. That's good."

It worked out that the pride had their spring break the same week Remi did, so the kids would all be able to hang out and entertain each other. Remi crossed her arms around her waist. There might be fallout from letting Greer's nieces and nephews mix with the pride—they'd have a ton of interesting questions about the watchers, the Friends, the Omnis, all of it.

Maybe this wasn't such a good idea. It was a bad suggestion on Owen's part to bring his family here instead of having the four of them go out to Ohio. Remi supposed he was just trying to show Greer's family that no one was a devil worshipper here.

But maybe they were, given the organization they were up against…and the secrets they had to keep.

"They're here," Val said, giving her a fortifying nod.

Remi followed Val and Ace into the foyer, her stomach feeling tighter and tighter.

Ace elbowed her. "Just don't hurl all over Greer's parents, okay? Not his sisters, either. Barf on Greer if you can aim at all."

"Ugh." Remi grinned. "Claim them. They're yours too. Why am I so nervous?"

"Because you're gonna be a Dawson soon."

That shocked the hell out of Remi. Before she could respond, the door opened and all kinds of chaos spilled into the house. Children. Adults. Greer with his parents. Max.

Greer looked for Remi first. He had a wide smile on his face. Even the tension that was usually in his eyes had eased up. He was happy about this visit. So often, he'd mentioned to Remi how he felt like an outsider even to his own family. Maybe that was just a misperception he'd been harboring. This crew looked excited and happy to be here. The kids were clearly wowed by the sprawling house. Wait until they got the tour in the morning.

After that thought, there wasn't another quiet moment. Remi got caught up in the chaos as everyone was introduced to everyone. Greer was by her side when his parents came over. His mom looked like she might burst out in tears. She clasped Remi's hands in both of hers.

"I am so very happy to finally to meet you," Blithe said.

Reed, Greer and Ace's dad, gave her a smile. "The heck with a handshake—I want a hug."

Remi's mind was spinning with all the new faces and names. Years of teaching had helped her develop tricks for remembering them, but she'd need at least one more day. What made matters worse was that Greer's sisters were twins, with the same shade of blue eyes—regular, blue eyes. Fortunately, their different haircuts helped distinguish them.

She looked around for Max, but he had slipped away.

"Greer, why don't we get everyone settled?" Remi asked. "You guys are on eastern time, so it's after midnight for you."

Greer nodded. "Good idea. Val, give me hand with the luggage." Between them and the two brothers-in-law, they wrangled the luggage upstairs, leaving some of the kids' things in the foyer. Everyone followed them. Grandma Blithe reminded the kids to be quiet, since the rest of their uncle and aunt's friends were asleep.

Remi smiled. The couples were probably not sleeping, but they had surrendered the house so Ace and Greer could welcome their family without the complication of meeting the bigger team. There would be plenty of time for that tomorrow.

"This place is huge," Tina said. "I can't wait to have a full tour."

Nancy, the younger twin, agreed. "And we want to hear all about everything you've been up to, Greer. I can't believe it's been so long since we caught up." She took Ace's hands. "And Ace, our baby sister. We can't wait to get to know you."

"It has been too long," Greer said. "And honestly, were it not for Ace and Remi, I'd probably still be an absent brother."

They deposited their luggage in the three spare rooms, one of which Remi used for an office. She'd tidied up her desk and put as much away as she could so Greer's parents could have the space for the next week. She did still have some papers to grade, but she'd moved those into the room she shared with Greer.

"Where are we going to sleep, Uncle Greer? Still in the basement?" Karen, the oldest of the nieces and nephews, asked.

"Yup. We have a group of kids living with us, so we have two big bunkrooms down there, but you'll have your own space for the week."

"Why are the kids living with you?" Billy asked.

"They are a special group who were taken from their families when they were young. They're staying here while we search for their parents."

Remi caught the concerned look the adults shared. Yeah, this week was going to be interesting. The team's work and living arrangements were unconventional, to say the least. Explaining it to the conventional world wouldn't be easy. Perhaps it was best to act as if it were the norm so its oddity didn't stick out so much.

No wonder Greer had been nervous about having his family out.

"How old are they?" Linda asked.

"How many of them are there?" Karen asked.

Greer sent Remi a panicked look. She smiled. His nieces and nephews were crowded around him. Two of them were holding his hands. Geez, the sight of him with kids melted something inside her. "Everything will make sense in the morning when you get to meet the other kids," Remi said. "It's their spring break too, so you'll have lots of time to play with them."

"If you guys are set here, why don't we head down to the kids' bunkroom and get the older ones situated?" Ace said.

The six adults weren't letting the kids out of their sight. The whole group followed Greer down the main stairs, then down the hallway to the basement stairs.

"We need to leave a trail of breadcrumbs so the kids can find their way back to our rooms," Seth said, not entirely joking.

"From where the kids will be, your rooms are just up the basement stairs, then up the main stairs and to the left. They'll find you," Ace said.

Remi was wondering if Ace was struck by how protected and loved these kids were. Her own hard-scrabble childhood had had her living in a maze of tunnels in King's Warren. If the differences had occurred to Ace, she didn't seem in the least resentful. She'd come a long way since her early days with the group, but then, she'd always been protective of children.

In the basement, they went toward the north end, where the girls' bunkroom was. Six bunks had been made. Like on the boys' side, there was a bathroom and an extra bedroom where a caretaker might sleep.

"Seriously, this is a maze. How do any of you find your way through all these rooms?" Nancy asked.

Greer and Ace exchanged a look. "Repetition," Ace said.

"I love it!" Karen said, claiming one of the upper bunks before the others could grab it.

The kids ran around the bunkroom, getting familiar with its spaces. Ace showed them the bathroom on that end of the basement.

OWL TUGGED ON HIS HOODIE, burrowing deeper into its cover. The kids that Ace and Greer had brought to the basement were about his age. They weren't well trained as watchers—they were noisy as hell. Some adults were with them. Their parents? Watchers didn't have parents. Maybe the adults were going to leave the kids here, but these new kids were kind of old to be joining a pride.

Greer opened the door to the girls' wing. He stood aside to let everyone enter, then looked back. Owl ducked out of view just in time. The classroom wall that ran adjacent to the hall was half glass. The group had flipped the lights on when they came down, destroying Owl's cover. He waited for Greer to follow the group into the girls' area before moving to a closer classroom. He wondered if the adults were going to stay with the kids.

He hoped not.

Ace, Greer, Remi, Val, and the older adults went upstairs. There was a flurry of activity as the kids got settled for the night. Some of them sounded whiney.

Watchers never whined, no matter how tired or hungry or hot or cold or hurt or lost or anything.

Owl moved even closer to the girls' bunkroom while the kids were in the bathroom, but he couldn't get inside because the two men were in there sitting on a couple of the lower bunks. Instead, he lingered in the nearby caretaker's bedroom.

"Nice accommodations Greer has here," one of them said.

"Yeah, but it makes me even more curious about Nancy's brother. What do we really know about him?"

"True. Tina doesn't know much either. And really, they don't talk a lot on the phone. Nor do they email. She said Greer's not on social media at all. Nor is Candace—Ace."

"And Ace is another can of worms. Do they know for a fact that she's a sibling? They thought she died when she was a baby."

"They never found her body."

"But did they do a DNA test? I've heard of stories of hucksters impersonating long-lost loved ones."

"Blithe said Greer had told them he had DNA run. Maybe we should grab material for our own DNA analysis."

"What does Greer do, anyway? This is a pretty swanky operation for a kid his age."

"Dunno. Guess that's what this weekend's for— getting to know each other more. He was in the Army when Tina and I got married."

"Same for Nancy and me. I knew she had a brother, but not much more than that. We didn't go to that party her parents threw him when he got out of the service and came here to work. Wish I had. It was last minute, and we had plans we couldn't get out of."

"We've got a week now to get to know the second half of the family. Gotta admit, I'm a little concerned. Greer and Ace are…I don't know. Odd?"

"Yeah, but their other halves seem normal. Things will be less weird in the morning. It's the shadows that set me on edge."

One of the men laughed. "We're such cowards."

"Speak for yourself. Me, I'm just suitably cautious."

The women brought the kids back into the bunkroom and got them settled for the night, then the adults went upstairs.

7

While the parents got their kids settled for the night, Greer brought his family into the kitchen. They sat around the cozy kitchen table. Russ and Jim had left a fire going. Greer added a couple of small logs and stoked it up again.

"Are you hungry?" Remi asked. "I could make up some sandwiches. Or maybe something to drink? Tea, hot chocolate? Maybe a hot toddy?"

Blithe smiled. "Oh, I like the sound of a hot toddy, Remi. Can I help you with that?"

"Nope. Stay put. I'll get the whiskey." She left Greer to visit with his parents while she went to the bar in the living room. Took a minute, but she found a bottle of Balcones. Hopefully, Owen wouldn't mind. And if he did, she'd buy him another.

In the kitchen, Greer saw the bottle. He gave a little shake of his head. Yeah, Owen probably would mind. Too bad. Val took the bottle from her.

"Don't worry," he whispered, bending close, "I'll replace it with one from my stash."

She got the hot water on while he squeezed some lemons. She searched for the spice cabinet, then found the cinnamon sticks, glad Russ kept his kitchen fully stocked.

"So how many people live here, son?" Reed asked.

"Hmm. I've sort of lost count," Greer said. "Russ and Jim, our cook and housekeeper, live in the guest house. There's eleven of us on the team, plus our significant others, so twenty, except Selena and Bastion are down in Colorado right now. Then the kids. Fourteen in the pride, if you count the two off at the community college in Colorado and don't include Beetle. Plus the four kids not in the pride. So what's that? Thirty-six living in the house right now?"

"Shit," Val said from the other side of the counter. "We are past capacity. Greer, you and Remi need to move out."

Reed and Blithe looked stunned. "So many," she said.

"And you all work in security?" Reed asked.

"The original team does," Greer said. "And Ace and Selena. The others do different things. Remi's an assistant professor of sociology at the University of Wyoming. Ivy owns a diner in town. Eddie has a dog-training business. Mandy runs a hippotherapy center. Hope's a mechanic. Addy runs a small greenhouse operation. Wynn's a teacher and nanny. Fiona's still at the university in Colorado."

"Wow." Blithe looked at Reed. She seemed overwhelmed.

Remi brought over their hot toddies. "Think of this place like a big apartment building. We really all just do our own thing. But we share meals, as we can."

"And all those kids?" Blithe asked. "You mentioned a pride. What's that?"

"You know," Remi said as she took a seat at the table, "without getting into details that aren't pertinent, the kids were part of a cult. They were very young when they were separated from their parents. The team's looking for their families, but finding them is proving difficult. They've lived together for a long time now—so long that they are a close-knit family. I almost hope we don't find their parents until they're adults, because separating them would be difficult. We've gotten them into the mainstream public school system, so they're slowly adapting to life outside the cult." She smiled at Greer. "I'm very proud of them. They're making a great transition."

Reed set his arms on the table and leaned toward Greer. "I just need to know one thing. I'm going to ask it, and you're probably going to get mad."

Remi reached over to set her hand on Greer's forearm.

Reed spit it out. "You *are* working within the law, right?"

Greer held his father's gaze a long moment before a slight grin curved his mouth. "Of course."

Remi elbowed Greer, knowing he resented the fear

his parents always held when considering him and his work. The way he'd just responded was a huge clue that he consciously or unconsciously seeded that fear himself.

"Yes, the team's work is legal," Remi said. "They work closely with the FBI and other law enforcement resources."

Before his parents could drill into that a bit more, Greer's sisters and their husbands came into the kitchen. "I hope it's all right that we left some lights on in the basement," Nancy said. "We didn't want it to be too dark for the kids if they need to come upstairs to find us."

"That's fine," Greer said. "I'll put the hallway lights in your wing on dim, too."

"Oh! Hot toddies!" Tina said, handing her sleeping daughter off to her husband, who already held an arm around their sleeping toddler. "Could I beg you for one?"

"You bet," Val replied, taking orders for refills from the group.

OWL STAYED in place a few more minutes, listening for sounds coming from behind the closed bunkroom door. When he didn't hear anything else, he returned to the pride's bunkroom with the news that the kids they'd been waiting for had arrived.

Crow and Badger were the ones in charge when Lion and Hawk were away. Owl wished Lion was still there, but Crow was doing a pretty good job of running things.

The two boys shared a bunk, Badger on the lower one, Crow up top. Owl climbed the ladder.

"Crow."

"What?"

"We've been infiltrated. The new pride is in the other bunkroom."

Crow sat up. He looked at Owl, blinked, then frowned. "How many?"

"Five, but only three are sleeping down here."

"Why didn't they introduce themselves?"

"Dunno. What should we do?"

"Get them before they get us. Wake the others."

Owl jumped down and told Badger, then went around to alert the other boys. This was serious. Trouble was inside their own home. Those watchers needed to learn a lesson.

The kids rolled out of their bunks and slipped into their night-ops clothes—black hoodies and jeans. They'd practiced moving all over the house in the middle of the night, being wherever they needed to be to guard the household. There were plenty of hiding places downstairs in the various classrooms, bedrooms, bathrooms, closets, and other nooks and crannies.

Most of them left their room and spread out into the dark corners of the basement. Crow and Badger stayed to guard their own bunkroom.

Owl found a spot inside one of the closets, climbing up to sit in the back corner of a shelf. They had orders not to engage unless they heard Crow's shout, so all he could do was wait—not his favorite thing, but it was something he was very good at.

KAREN LAY in the dark in her bunk, listening to the sounds of the unfamiliar place. Their room had recently been cleaned—she could tell by how fresh the blankets smelled. Everything was tidy and new. And yet...something was off. This place was off. What kind of home had so much space? It wasn't a hotel. Or a YMCA hostel, like she'd stayed at once in the sixth grade.

Uncle Greer had said for them to keep quiet so as not to disturb the kids sleeping at the other end of the basement.

Who were those kids? Why did they live in a spooky basement when there were so many other rooms upstairs?

Karen leaned over the edge of her bunk and hissed at her sister in the one beneath her. "Psst. Linda. Wake up."

"I'm not sleeping."

"I can't sleep either. Want to go exploring?"

"Yes." Linda sat up.

"Get your phone. We'll use our lights." Karen quietly climbed down from her bunk, phone in hand. "Don't turn your light on until we're out of the room. Don't want to wake Billy."

"Where are you going?" Billy asked.

"Shh." Karen put her finger against her lips. "We're just going to the bathroom. We'll be right back."

"I need to pee, too," Billy said.

Linda gave a dramatic sigh. "We're not peeing."

"Ew. Couldn't you have done that before?" he asked.

"Just stay put. We'll be right back," Karen ordered him.

"No. I'm going with you. You might get lost."

"We're not going to get lost," Linda said.

"There could be secret passageways. This place is huge," Billy replied.

Karen huffed. "Fine. Come with us. Just quit talking before you wake the kids at the other end of the basement."

The three of them tiptoed out of their bunkroom and into the dark hallway that led past another bedroom, the bathroom, then several different rooms that had half-glass walls facing the hallway.

"What a weird place," Karen whispered as they walked around the different rooms. They looked like classrooms. Were the kids in the other bunkroom the students who were taught here? Were they kept a secret in this place?

All sorts of alarms were ringing in her mind. Not to mention the place was filled with shadows that seemed to move. She kept catching faint sounds.

She turned to the others with her and cautioned them to silence. "I hear something," she whispered.

"What?" Billy asked.

"Let her listen, stupid," Linda said.

"Both of you, hush!" Karen held still. She even paused her breathing. When she drew her next breath, she tried to be quiet about it, but that just made her heart race.

It was worth it, though: that sound came again. It wasn't exactly a sound—more like a movement of air. Movement that shouldn't be happening given that no one but the three of them was out and about. There had been no sound coming from the closed doors of the other bunkroom. It was past midnight now—the other kids had to all be asleep.

Karen looked at Linda and Billy. Both of them appeared ready to jump out of their skins. "It's nothing," she said. "Go back if you're scared."

"We're not leaving you alone," Billy said.

Karen made a face. "Nothing's going to happen to us. Let's just finish exploring."

"When we're done here," Billy said, "want to go look around upstairs? Bet they have food in the kitchen."

Linda snorted. "Because it's a kitchen."

Karen walked out of the last classroom and headed toward the boys' bathroom. Billy stopped her.

"You can't go in there. It's the boys' bathroom."

"Billy, you went into the girls' bathroom."

"I'll check this one out," he said. "You two wait here."

Karen crossed her arms. "Fine. Do it."

They waited.

And waited.

And…no Billy.

Linda's eyes were wide with worry. "What happened to him?"

"I don't know." Karen couldn't call out for him without risking waking the other kids. Still, she quietly said, "Billy? Billy? This isn't funny."

No response. Karen looked at her sister. "He's probably just trying to out-wait us. I'll go see what he's up to."

Linda grabbed her sleeve. "He'll probably try to scare you."

Karen chuckled. "I know."

She went into the boys' bathroom. The lights were out. She flipped the switch, but nothing happened. At least she had her phone light. "Billy," she hissed, "where are you?"

She knew this bathroom had to be a duplicate of the girls' bathroom at their end of the basement, but in the dark, the shadows stretched and twisted, moving in weird ways as she panned her phone about. All of the stalls were half open. She ducked and looked for feet, but didn't see any.

She moved deeper into the long room, going over to the shower area. The curtains at each stall were open. No Billy in any of them. It was there, deep inside the bathroom, that she heard a muffled cry. She hurried toward the sound. "Billy? Linda? You guys, knock it off. This isn't funny. I'm going to tell Mom and Aunt Tina."

She held still and kept quiet as she stood near the hallway door. Nothing. She pulled the door open and stepped back into the hallway. Linda was gone.

Karen turned her phone down both ends of the long hallway. The door to the girls' bunkroom was still closed. But not the boys' bunkroom. It was open, showing nothing but a dark span beyond it.

She had a choice—she could run for the stairs and try to make it up to her parents, two levels above, or she could go into the boys' bunkroom after her sister. And who knew where Billy was—he couldn't have gotten out of the bathroom without going past Linda. Maybe he got out while she was back in the shower area.

Karen gave a last look at the stairs, then went after her sister. She crept toward the boys' bunkroom. Just inside the doorway, she paused to flip the lights on, but here, too, they weren't working. She sent her phone's light spilling through the room. The bunks looked occupied. She couldn't see anyone awake—not from the doorway, at least.

Cautiously, she moved deeper into the room. There were more bunks in here than in the girls' bunkroom. These weren't lined up against the wall—they stuck out perpendicular to it.

She got to the last row of bunks and found her sister tied to a chair, her mouth gagged. Two boys stood behind her. Linda started to squeal frantically.

Yeah. Time to get the grownups.

She pivoted, but before she could get through the room, boys rolled out of their bunks, spilling like rats from shelves.

Karen opened her mouth and screamed and screamed. Her legs went weak. Never in her life had she been so scared. She squeezed her phone, hitting the panic button app Uncle Greer had installed on all of their phones. One of the boys knocked her phone from her hand, then dragged her over to a chair next to the other. In only seconds, her feet were bound to the legs, her hands were tied behind her, and a gag was shoved in her mouth.

GREER'S ALARM went off at about the same time he heard screams coming from the hallway. He jumped out of bed and banged on Ace and Val's door. The alarm had come from Karen's phone, which was showing as still in the basement. Whatever had frightened her had sent one or more of the kids screaming up the stairs.

Billy was already slamming through his parents' door as Greer and Ace were charging down the stairs to the basement, Remi and Val close on his heels. Greer was vaguely aware of the rest of his team spilling out into the hallway, along with his parents and sisters and their husbands.

All kinds of terrible thoughts spilled through Greer's mind in the seconds it took to go down two flights of stairs. Max was locking down the house—Greer could hear the automatic shades closing and the windows locking. Those shades were a new addition to the fortifications around Blade's house, and Greer was glad they had them in place.

No lights worked in the basement. "I'll check the

breakers," Ace whispered.

She got the power restored just as Greer walked into the boys' open bunkroom door. Light flooded the room. The boys were standing around the chairs where his nieces were restrained. The girls were close to hysterical.

"Untie them, Crow."

"Yes, sir."

The boys got their knives out and made short work of the restraints. As soon as they were free, the girls ran out of the bunkroom and up the stairs, passing Ace on their way.

Greer gave each boy a stare-down. "What's going on?"

Before the boys could answer, Ace touched his arm. "Hold off on the inquisition. Owen wants to do it." She had a finger pressed against the comm unit in her ear; he'd forgotten his.

"Shit." He looked at the boys and shook his head. Of all the times for them to act up, this was not a good one.

"Yeah, he wants them brought to the living room." Ace turned her back on the boys to hide the grin she gave Greer. "Guess the family's all there, along with the whole fucking household."

"Shit, shit, shit." He shoved his fingers through his hair and looked at the boys. "You better have a good explanation ready."

"Your nieces and nephews have strong lungs," Ace said as she and Greer followed the boys upstairs.

"*Our* nieces and nephews, Ace. Yours and mine." He

just hoped whatever the reason the boys had terrified the kids made some kind of sense—and that Tina and Nancy would be as amused as Ace was.

"Right."

Upstairs, there was a lot of chatter going on. The girls were still crying, though now it was mostly whimpers and long, shaky breaths. The whole team, their significant others, the pride, and Greer's family were in the living room.

Owen looked pissed. The women looked scared. His dad was furious.

Well, wasn't that just fuckbuckets full of fun.

Owen put his hands behind his back. "Care to tell me what's going on?" he asked Greer.

"No idea. Crow, front and center," Greer said.

Crow stepped forward. His face was stoic. Whatever had happened, he and the pride had been planning it.

"Let's have it," Greer said. "Why have you ganged up on my nieces and nephew?"

"They're your real nieces and nephew?" Crow asked.

Greer tilted his head as he tried to process that. "Um. Far as I know."

Crow looked back at the boys. "We thought they were watchers."

"I told you my family was coming."

"Yeah, but we're your family too. You're all like uncles and aunts to us. I thought you meant you were bringing in more watchers. We were just establishing dominance—you know, a pecking order for things."

Greer rubbed his hand over his face, stalling for a

few seconds before having to deal with this. "I see."

"Was anyone hurt?" Owen asked as he looked the visiting kids over.

Karen straightened and swiped her wrist across her face. "They only won because we didn't know they'd shut down the power."

Owen's brows rose. "Were. You. Hurt?"

"No, sir," Karen said. She looked at Linda and Billy. They also said they were fine.

"It's scary down there without lights," Billy said.

"Who are these kids, Greer, and why have you put our kids next to dangerous hoodlums?" Greer's dad asked.

"The pride's not dangerous," Greer said.

"We are too," Crow said.

"Not now, Crow," Max warned him.

"So, given the circumstance," Greer said to his family, "maybe I should have had you arrive in the morning, not at night. I thought these introductions could hold off until the morning, but looks like now's the time to make them." Greer introduced his family to Owen and the rest of the team. He nodded toward the boys. "That's the group of kids we mentioned when we were talking earlier. They are our family—we are their uncles and aunts. I'm sorry they got the wrong notion about the rest of the kids." He looked at Crow. "For the record, any children who visit here—whether blood relatives or rescues or other watchers—are always to be treated as honored guests. We will establish the pecking order, not you."

"Understood." Crow looked at the now-recovered kids. "Sorry about scaring you."

Karen blushed. "It wasn't so bad."

"You could scream the ears off a screech owl," Crow said.

"They don't have ears—not outside ones, anyway," Billy said. Karen giggled.

Owen looked at Greer, who had no answers. None. He just wanted to put this night behind him.

"Well, now that's settled," Russ said, standing next to Jim on the top step in the dining room, "how about some hot chocolate for everyone?"

The kids all shouted in the affirmative and rushed behind him into the kitchen.

"We saw the lights on all over the house and thought we'd come see what was going on," Jim said.

Greer hadn't even noticed that Max had reversed the lockdown. A cool hand slipped into his. Remi was smiling up at him. "I think that went better than it might have."

Greer shook his head. "I think I should have been clearer with the pride."

"Probably, but who would have expected a challenge their very first night here?"

Owen came over to stand with them as the room emptied out. "Your niece Karen is tough. Maybe there's room for her in the family business in the future."

"No." Greer shook his head. "Not happening. She's why we do what we do, O. I wouldn't wish this career on anyone."

Owen nodded. "Fair enough."

Greer's mom came over to them. She smiled as she hugged Greer. "Well, that was certainly startling, honey."

"It was. Sorry about that, Mom. Our boys haven't been around visitors here much."

His mom drew back and, putting an arm around Remi, asked Owen, "Is it always so eventful here?"

Owen shook his head. "Not in the least." Even his smile didn't give away the lie. "I'm going to hit the sack, but I'll ask Russ to hold breakfast a little later in the morning so everyone can sleep in."

"Oh, no need to do that! We'll be up when Greer gets up. I don't want to waste a minute of our time together."

"Right. Good night, then." Owen reached a hand out to Addy. They left together.

Crow came up to the small group. "I just want to say I'm sorry. That got out of hand fast. Lion wouldn't have messed up like that."

"Lion's four years older than you," Greer said. "I bet he messed up plenty of times." Greer held his hand out, palm up. "But can you at least give me back the years you ripped from my life tonight?"

Crow laughed. Remi squeezed Greer's hand. And his mother smiled at Crow with her warm eyes, looking as if she had a new grandson.

The night was weird as hell, but it was also kind of nice.

8

The next morning was like any weekend morning after a night spent bingeing on horror flicks: Greer was still fighting an anxiety hangover—and was relieved as hell that his family hadn't called for a ride down to the Cheyenne airport. His tension only deepened the closer he came to the main living room and the adjacent dining room.

Whatever he'd been expecting, it wasn't what he found when he got there. His mom was sitting at the long dining room table, surrounded by the pride, her own grandkids, and the kids belonging to Kit, Owen, and Rocco. She was telling them some story from her own childhood, which held them in rapt attention.

Greer cocked his head as he watched his mom work her magic. The pride had bonded with several elderly Friends who had helped support them with clothes, blankets, and food. But the kids had rarely had the luxury of hearing an elder storyteller. His mom was loving the attention just as much as the kids were.

A woman's arm went around his waist. At first, Greer thought Remi had joined him, but the woman was too tall and her perfume was unfamiliar. He turned to see Nancy smile at him.

She jerked her chin toward the kids in the dining room. "I guess all is forgiven."

Greer chuckled. "Things are always more horrifying at night. Sorry it got so out of hand. I expected a less competitive reaction from the boys. Hopefully, they learned their lesson."

"Maybe. But no real harm was done. And standing on this side of it, it's kinda funny. Dad was pissed, though." She laughed. "Haven't seen him like that since we were growing up."

"Yeah. Anger was his go-to emotion for me."

Nancy gave him a squeeze. "Not so anymore. He's damned proud of you, even if he can't quite grasp what it is that you do." She paused. "What do you do?"

"Computer stuff, mostly. Hacking enemy systems."

"Nothing illegal, though, right?"

He paused just long enough to put his answer in question. "Yeah. Right. Obvs."

Tina came up and joined them, hugging Greer from his other side. "I love it here! Any chance we can get the full tour?"

"Sure. After everyone's had breakfast." Greer looked at the table of kids and his mom. "Hey, Case—feel like leading a tour around the property in a little bit?"

"Sure, Uncle Greer," Casey said. "Can I show them the bunker?"

Greer pretended to be shocked she'd mentioned it. Truthfully, seeing their secret workspace might help his family put their fears to rest. "Well I guess we have to now, seeing as you mentioned it and all. We'll go after everyone's had breakfast." He looked at his mom. "It's a big place. You're going to need your strength."

"That is unnerving," she said. He grinned at her.

"But seriously, what are we going to do today?" Nancy asked.

"Your choice," Greer replied. "We could take a hike. Or go for a horseback ride — if Mandy doesn't have any customers."

"All of us?" Steve asked as he brought steaming coffee mugs over for him and Tina.

Greer indicated the family group. "The kids, Ace, Val, Remi, and I have spring break. Everyone else is working this week."

"Um, Greer," Nancy said, "it's snowing outside, so maybe outdoor things can wait for better weather."

"Right. We could watch a movie in the theater room. You could work out in the gym. Maybe some quiet time for reading. The kids have a ton of games we could play. Or we could go swimming."

"Swimming!" several of the kids shouted together.

"Swimming it is," Greer said. "There's a hot tub for the adults. Great place to warm up on a day like this."

EVERYONE MET in the foyer an hour later. Remi set her hand in Greer's and smiled at him. For the life of him, Greer couldn't understand how he lucked into finding a woman like her.

Ace elbowed him. "Casey's got a question for you."

"Oh. Sorry, Case."

"Where should we start the tour?" Casey asked.

"Let's start upstairs," Greer said.

Casey led the way up the main stairs, hurrying to keep ahead of the rush of kids. The adults brought up the rear.

"Where's Val?" Greer asked Ace.

"He's staying back to get a pitcher of margaritas and some snacks ready for the pool." She grinned. "I know you said the house was ours this week and everyone was staying out of our hair, but it seems the spring break mood has hit everyone. I think the pool's going to be the most crowded it's ever been."

Greer nodded. "I like that."

"Uncle Greer," Casey called over to him. "Can I show them the attics?"

"Sure. Go for it." Greer looked at his parents. "It's just attics. Feel free to go up if you like, but we can wait here for the kids."

Blithe put her hand in Greer's. "Thanks for having us all out for a visit. I'm really enjoying myself. Dad is too."

Greer put his arm around his mom's shoulders and gave her a sideways hug. "It hasn't even begun. And it got off to a rocky start last night."

"It's a memory that will make me chuckle for a long time."

Greer kissed her temple. "Love you, Mom."

When the kids were finished with the first attic, they ran up to the second. After that, they walked to the end of each wing. Greer and Ace let the kids go into their rooms in the southern bedroom wing.

Then they toured the public rooms downstairs. The kids loved the theater room. The adults loved the wine room and the billiards room. The gym wing was a big hit with the whole group. His mom was convinced he and Ace lived in a resort.

"We work long hours sometimes," Greer said. "It can be hard to get time off, so having these things is a nice plus."

"Now the bunker, Uncle Greer?" Casey asked.

"Sure. But wait in the den until we're all there."

"What is it you all do here, exactly?" Greer's dad asked.

"We're special consultants to the Department of Homeland Security," Greer said. "We help in the fight against terrorists, domestic and foreign."

They reached the den. It was a tight fit with his family, the kids, and pride all stuffed in the room. Max was waiting for them.

"Can we go in?" Casey asked.

"Not yet," Max said, his rumbling voice rising above the noise of the group. "I need you all to sign a nondisclosure agreement."

"Oh, get real, Max," Ace grumbled.

Max looked at her with his hard eyes. "Have you ever known me to be a jokester, Ace?"

Greer was handing out papers to sign. It was a copy of a handwritten statement: the signer vowed to never divulge what they were about to see, under penalty of the worst punishment Uncle Greer could devise.

Remi chuckled when she read it.

"Only the newcomers need to sign it," Max said, winking at Ace.

"I guess that's us," Blithe said. She signed her copy and left it on the desk.

When the papers were all signed and stacked, Max went into the closet and opened the secret door. Greer's nieces and nephews looked spooked. They'd gone quiet and were bunched close to each other.

"Is this safe, dear?" Blithe asked Greer.

"Sure. Just go slowly. Kids—stop at the bottom of the stairs."

Reed sent him a dark look.

"The bunker was put in when the house was built. It was a Cold War-era bug-out spot. When a later owner added the bedroom wings, he extended the bunker to the south. Is it overkill? Yes. But on the other hand, it's given us space for our work." Greer left out the nitty-gritty history of the bunker and house. Keeping it simple and fairly close to the truth was best for now.

Max unlocked the door into the conference room. The group spilled into that cavernous space. When some of the kids headed toward the hallway at the back,

Max's piercing whistle stopped them. "Let's stay together."

"We have our team meetings in here," Greer said.

"Where we plan for world domination events," Ace added.

Greer took them down the hall, pausing by the kitchen, bathroom, bunkroom, and ops room. The door to the weapons room was closed—and locked.

"What's in that room?" Steve asked.

"Supplies," Greer said. The ops room wasn't large enough to accommodate everyone, so people came in and left. His parents were the last in the group. "This is where I spend most of my time. Max, too."

Blithe smiled. "I always knew this was what you wanted to do."

"And technical stuff came easily to you," Reed said. "Glad you found your niche."

"Thanks, guys," Greer said.

"Hey, Uncle Greer—were does that door go?" Karen asked, pointing to the double steel doors at the tunnel entrance.

Greer looked at Max. "Well, no good bug-out spot is worth anything if there isn't an escape hatch. Open it and see."

Max unlocked it. Karen and Linda opened the doors to the raised loading dock. The kids spilled out that way.

"Where does that lead?" Seth asked.

"Out to the side of the house," Ace said.

"I'll show you," Max said.

"It's a bit of a hike," Greer told his parents.

"I think I'm good," Blithe said. "I want to go up and get ready for the pool."

"I'm going to see where it leads," Reed said. "See you at the pool in a bit."

Seth and Steve swapped glances. "We're going too."

Blithe, Remi, Ace, and Greer stayed behind, while everyone else followed Max into the tunnel. They returned to the den. Greer noticed that his mom drew a big breath.

"It's a little claustrophobic down there, don't you think?" Blithe asked Greer.

"I guess it could be. I'm usually too busy working to notice." He reached for Remi's hand. "I'm going to see if Val needs any help. Why don't guys go get ready for the pool? Jim has already put some towels down there, so you won't need to bring any from your rooms. Just watch the kids if they're in the big pool."

"Wynn said she'd be a lifeguard for us," Remi said.

"Good. I don't know how well the kids can swim." Swimming had been one of the first survival things Greer's grandfather had taught him. It hit him then, how different his own childhood was from what Nancy and Tina experienced, and what their children were living. No one in the next generation was stepping into the life he and Ace had been groomed for.

He hoped it stayed that way.

Greer found Val in the billiards room. They exchanged a tense look.

"This is good," Greer said. "It needs to happen. I spoke to my mom before the tour. She's on board with a spontaneous meeting with Ace. She was trying to figure out how to do this herself. What happens now is up to Ace."

Giving Ace and Blithe a quiet moment together was the very thing Rocco's counselor had suggested—that and going in with no set expectations. If they even came a step closer after their chat, then it should be considered a win.

"I mentioned it to Ace this morning," Val said. "I didn't want her to be broadsided. She's gotten better about calling your family hers, but I think that's still in the abstract for her."

"She's good with it?"

"I think so. Although, if she could just let it be for the rest of her life, she would."

"True. But that's why she has us. I'm going to go get my mom."

9

A knock sounded on Ace and Val's bedroom door. She flashed an angry look at Val, then hurried into the closet.

"Just a minute," he called as he followed her.

Ace ignored him. She pulled on a pair of gray yoga pants over her bikini bottoms, then yanked a hoodie off a shelf. Too late, she realized it was Val's. He'd worn it a couple of times, and it still smelled like him. She drew that delicious scent into her lungs, not even bothering to hide that motion from him.

"It's not like you to hide," Val said.

"It's not like you to gang up on me."

"Blithe's your mom. No one's ganging up on you."

"I don't want a mom. I don't want Greer's family. He can keep them."

"That's not reality, SweeTart."

"It could have been. It should have been. I should never have gone with Greer to meet them."

"That still wouldn't have changed reality. You are their daughter."

Ace shook her head, angry that tears were distorting her vision. "I don't want to dredge everything up. I don't want to tell them what happened to me. I don't want any of this, Val." She huffed a breath. "Please."

He pulled her into his arms, flattening her against him. She let one broken sob out, then stopped breathing, trying to get a grip on herself. "Get rid of my mom." Her words were muffled against his chest. "I don't want to see her when I leave."

"No. No more running. No more hiding. No more avoiding. You don't have to dredge up the past. You don't have to say anything about anything. Pretend your life started today."

"She's going to ask questions."

"Nope. Greer and I prepped her to stay present and start from here."

"I can't do this, Val. Don't make me."

"I'm not making you do anything. Your mom wants a visit with you."

"I don't *have* a mom."

"I've never known you to be cruel, SweeTart. Put yourself in your mom's shoes."

"No."

"She lost her baby girl. Mourned her for over two decades. Then had a miracle dropped in her lap when her baby was returned to her."

"I'm not a baby. And I'm not a miracle."

"To her you are. Just start here. Now. Today. There

is no yesterday. And the future is entirely up to you." Val took hold of her shoulders. "God, Ace. If I could have this chance with my mom, if she one day showed up like Owen's Addy and his dad did—I'd be on my knees thanking all the powers that be."

A fat, hot tear dropped down Ace's cheek. She swiped it away.

"I'll stay if you want me to."

Ace shook her head.

"I love you," Val said.

"I hate you."

He laughed. "No you don't."

"Go away."

"Call me if you need me."

Val left. Ace stayed in the closet for a long moment that turned into a couple of minutes, almost too long. Too fucking bad there wasn't a back way out of there.

Her mom had come in when Val left—Ace knew she was quietly waiting for her.

She opened the closet door and stepped just to the doorjamb. Her mom was sitting in one of the side chairs. Her dad was not with her. That was a relief. Somehow, this was easier with just her mom.

Ace lifted heavy eyes to her mom's kind ones, wondering where to start. "Sorry I made you wait."

Her mom gave Ace a smile and said, "I would wait forever for you."

Tears again flooded Ace's eyes. "I can't do this."

"Do what?"

"Start today. Here. Now."

Her mom nodded. "I don't know how to do this either. I just know that not confronting it is as hard as not having you when I know you're alive and you survived."

"I don't want to talk about anything that happened."

"Done."

"I don't want to talk about lost time."

"Done. Tell me about Val."

"I love him."

Blithe nodded. "I think I do too. He has to be a strong man to stand beside you."

"Sometimes he's not beside me. Sometimes he can barely keep up."

"Good. Keep him on his toes. What do you think of your nieces and nephews?"

Ace shrugged. "Not at all sure. Never expected to have a whole ready-made family. They seem nice. But they could use a little training in stealth."

Blithe laughed. "They would love that. Your sisters, God bless them, are good people. Soft, but good. You and Greer, you are their opposites. Still good, but forged in fire. I'm proud of all of my babies, warriors and civilians. The world needs all kinds of people to keep it growing and evolving. I could never do what you and Greer do, but my dad did, and I don't imagine he came out of nowhere. Maybe strength like yours skips generations."

"Maybe it needs a rest now and then."

"Likely so." Blithe stood up and straightened her terrycloth swimsuit cover. "We will start today, and go from here."

Ace sighed. "Okay."

"Are you going to join us in the pool?"

"Yeah. I'll go down with you. Let me just put my tee on." She went over to the bed where she'd set out her shirt and towel. She pulled Val's hoodie off, then heard her mom gasp.

Her arms were already in the sleeves of her tee but she hadn't pulled it on yet. Her shoulders dipped as her mom came around to stand behind her.

"God, that's beautiful."

Ace bit back the tears. "You think so?"

"I never was much in favor of tattoos, but this is such beautiful art."

"Val said I am the butterfly I wear."

"He's a wise man."

Ace pulled her tee over her head. She knew her mom had seen her scars—she'd been watching Blithe in the mirror. But Blithe hadn't touched her back, leaving the seal of Ace's emotions somewhat intact.

"Ready to go swimming? Your nieces and nephews can't wait to have time with you. You're someone who's mysterious and badass. They're a little afraid and whole lot in awe of you."

"Badass. I can't believe you said that."

"Well, you are. And that badassery has kept you alive. So you just keep on being one."

Ace nodded. "It's the road I'm on. I haven't seen many off-ramps, as of yet."

Blithe's gaze was unwavering. "Do you want one?"

"No. I haven't seen one because I haven't been looking."

Her mom pulled her in for a surprise hug. It took Ace a long moment to wrap her arms around her mom in return.

"I love you," Blithe said. "And I'm proud of you. And I really hope you can swim, else your nieces and nephews will realize you're a mere mortal."

Ace laughed. She grabbed her pool towel and followed her mom from the room.

The noise from the open pool room doors hit them as they entered the gym wing. So much laughter. Blithe smiled at Ace. Val, Greer, his—her—brothers-in-law, and her dad weren't in the room. This family thing was going to take some getting used to.

Wynn was on lifeguard duty. Ace's sisters, Remi, Eddie, and Hope were all in the hot tub. Angel and Blade were in the big pool, swimming with the kids.

"C'mon, you two—join us!" Nancy called over to them.

"Val set us all up with margaritas, then left with Greer," Remi said.

Ace picked a spot near the hot tub to set her towel down. She stepped out of her yoga pants and then pulled her tee off, dropping it next to her towel and pants. The bikini she wore showed off her big blue swallowtail tattoo.

Her sisters gasped.

"That's gorgeous, Ace," Tina said. She looked at Nancy. "And you thought you were bold with your little ankle tat."

Nancy laughed. "I *was* bold with that!"

Remi got out to pour a margarita for Ace. She asked as she handed it to her, "You okay?"

Ace nodded. "I think so."

Tina and Nancy scooted apart. "Come sit with us."

Ace didn't hesitate to do that. They took turns admiring her ink up close. Ace didn't miss the surreptitious glances they sent Blithe. She sipped her margarita, surprised to realize her sisters' connection with Blithe didn't feel awful. In fact, knowing that her new family and her existing one had conspired to bring her into the fold felt a little amazing.

After a while, some of the other guys joined Angel and Blade in the big pool. Jim and Russ brought platters of food in for everyone to eat lunch in the pool room so they didn't have to stop playing long. Or, as was more likely, Jim didn't want to have to clean up after dozens of wet bodies went traipsing through the house to grab some food.

Val came in. She smiled at him, then got out of the hot tub to greet him. She didn't care who watched them—she was long past that minor concern. Everyone knew they were together. She just felt so small when he wrapped his arms around her.

"I love you." She leaned back to look up at him.

He raised his brows. "You sure about that? Last time I saw you, you said you hated me."

"I did. But now I love you."

"You are so fickle. I can barely keep up with you."

"That's what I told my mom."

Val went still. He studied her. "So it went okay?"

"It did."

"Good job."

Greer came by. He paused briefly next to them. "So...we good, li'l sis?"

Ace gave him a hug. "We're good."

Their brothers-in-law went past. Looking a little spooked by her, they didn't pause, just nodded a hello. Her dad was next. His heart was in his eyes. How hadn't she noticed that before?

Greer stepped aside, opening the circle to Reed. He held his arms out tentatively. Ace felt a wave of pressure building behind her eyes. Not knowing what else to do, she stepped into her dad's arms and leaned her head against his chest. He hugged her, curling around her as if she were a small child.

Neither of them had any words in that moment, so when the hug was over, they simply parted, each wiping the tears away. Reed put his arm around her shoulders and turned her to face the rest of their family.

"I'm glad we came," Reed said, looking at Blithe. "We haven't been together as a family in a long time."

Tina and Nancy crossed the hot tub to hug Blithe and Remi, then got out to give Ace, Greer, and then their dad hugs.

"Time to feed the monsters," Nancy said.

Several teak tables were set up around the pool. Wynn was already helping the pride get settled with their lunches. Ivy, Mandy, and Addy had followed Jim and Russ in, and they were doing the same with their kids.

THINGS WERE chaotic while everyone grabbed something to eat. The kids settled in various clusters. Tina and Nancy's husbands sat with Val and several of the guys. It always interested Remi to see how groups spontaneously organized themselves.

Greer gathered Remi and his parents, then led them over to the buffet.

"Your company has been treating us as if this were a five-star hotel," his mom said, wrapping her arm around his. "I feel so spoiled."

"Is it always like this?" Reed asked.

Greer exchanged smiles with Remi. "Pretty much. Jim and Russ do a great job of managing the household so all we have to do is focus on our work."

"That's a creampuff gig," his dad said, chuckling.

"And you two were worried about me and Ace."

"Not anymore!" his mom said.

After filling plates, the four of them joined Tina and Nancy. Remi looked around to see where Ace was, and found her over with Val.

"So, tell me everything about the two of you," Tina said, leaning over the table. Her eyes were sparkling with mischief.

Remi smiled and shot a quick glance at Greer, checking to see if he wanted to take that one. He nodded at her. "We met working on a case." Remi was pleased with her answer—it didn't divulge much, which also meant it hadn't satisfied Tina at all.

"She hated me at first," Greer said, laughing.

"No. Why?" Nancy asked.

"Well, he came in like a hurricane. I feared he was going to take my case away from me."

"What were you working on?" Tina asked.

Nancy prodded Tina. "If you can't say, it's fine."

"As a sociologist, I've focused my efforts on studying isolationist groups. In fact, I was offered positions at several universities across the country, but I chose the University of Wyoming specifically because of its proximity to one of these groups that most interest me—the Friendship Community."

"Remi has a master's from Stanford University and her doctorate from Princeton," Greer said—with a level of pride that warmed everything inside Remi.

"Goodness, you could have your pick of situations," Blithe said.

"I did."

"What made you choose sociology for your career?" Tina asked.

A wave of tension washed over Remi. She didn't like

talking about her background—she still felt so much shame around it. "I was born into an isolationist community—a polygamist group in southwestern Colorado. I think I picked my specialty as a way of healing from my childhood…and giving it all some perspective."

Nancy gave her a sympathetic look. "Wow. So it was a bad experience."

"Not when I was little. There were always a lot of kids to play with. There was plenty to eat. The community had a lot of structure. It wasn't until I hit puberty that things got strange. Girls were generally married by the time they were fourteen or fifteen. They weren't allowed to continue their education once they were married. And the curriculum the group followed was pure, twisted, religious propaganda at that point. We weren't taught anything of the current world outside our community. We weren't even taught about our state or nation. Everything was set to ensure our ignorance and compliance. At that young age, the elders considered us gifts from God. Sexual offerings, if you will. My mom got us out of there before anything happened to me, but my friends weren't so lucky."

Everyone at the table had stopped eating. It was all disgusting—she couldn't blame them for their reaction. Greer reached over and took her hand.

"Where is your mom now?" Blithe asked.

"She returned to the group when I went to college. She died shortly after that."

"Oh, my. You've been alone a long time."

Remi nodded. "Until Greer bulldozed his way into my life."

"So what was it that made you think he was going to interrupt your work?" Tina asked.

"In tracking our terrorists," Greer said, "we identified a group that was using Remi's group for their nefarious purposes. I wasn't certain that Remi wasn't part of what the bad guys were doing." He smiled at Remi. "At best, she looked like a roadblock, and yeah, we bulldoze those."

"So which one of you caved first?" Nancy asked.

"He did."

"She did."

Remi and Greer laughed. "Fine. It was me," Greer said.

"Once I saw a little crack in his armor, I saw he was more than just a hardass."

"Yeah, she pried that little crack wide open and climbed right in."

"And why wouldn't I? You were everything."

"Oh. My. God," Tina gasped, straightening. "Tell me you're getting married."

Nancy shoved her elbow into Tina's arm. Hard. "Of course they are. Sometime. The last thing they need is family pushing them."

Tina ignored what her sister had just said. "Why not do it while we're here?" She clapped her hands as if she couldn't contain the excitement. "I'm serious. We could help put it together. We could chip in on some catering. It could even be a pool party wedding!"

Remi giggled and looked to see what Greer's reaction was.

"We've already talked about getting married," he said.

"These things aren't simple events that can be easily thrown together," Blithe said. "Half the joy is in the planning. Let them set a date. We can all come back."

Greer gave her his most adorable boyish grin. "How about Friday?"

Remi's mouth made a wide O. "Are you serious?"

He nodded. "We could do Thursday. I don't want to wait to marry you."

Remi gripped the table as the room seemed to spin around her. Greer wanted to make a huge leap. With her. And his whole family was on board with bringing her into their group. Remi's eyes teared up.

Her hesitation had given Greer a look of near panic. She nodded. "Let's do it."

"When? Wednesday?" he asked.

She laughed. "Saturday. I want Lion, Hawk, and Fiona to be here."

Greer let out a whoop. He scooped Remi up and spun her around, spilling their chairs. He set her on her feet and kissed her like they were alone in the room. When they parted, Remi realized everyone had gone silent, watching them warily.

"We're getting married!" Greer shouted.

The room erupted in glee. Everyone made their way over to congratulate them. The joy Remi felt was more than she'd ever known. She kept stepping back mentally so that she could take it all in. She wanted to remember this forever.

Greer was the most wonderful gift she'd ever received.

"When's the big date?" Val asked.

"Saturday," Greer said.

"Saturday! Greer!" Ivy put a hand on her huge belly. "We'll make it happen."

"We have all the decorations here from the weddings a few months ago," Mandy said.

"We'll make it easy-ish," Nancy said. "I'm sure there's a place in town that can cater. We'll bring food in. We'll get some flowers and find a dress for Remi. You have two extra workers in me and Tina." Belatedly, she checked with the bride in question. "If that suits. It's all your call."

Remi laughed. "It all suits perfectly. Casual. Easy. Fun."

"Right," Ivy said. "We have less than a week. We better get started this afternoon."

"The good thing is that we have lots of experience planning weddings," Mandy said, laughing.

Greer pulled Remi into his arms. For a moment, the world narrowed to just him and her as she stared into his whiskey-brown eyes. "I love you."

"I love you."

"You can change your mind, you know."

"I don't want to."

"Then Saturday, you'll be Mrs. Dawson. Or Dr. Mrs. Chase-Dawson."

Remi laughed. "I don't think that's a real title. I'll have to figure that out. Some of my married colleagues have kept their maiden name at work but use their married name legally. I don't know."

"You have a week to figure that out!"

"I'm on it!"

10

It was strange driving down to Laramie on an off-work day, but the reason for doing so was exciting. Remi's gaze lingered on his profile as he drove. He caught her watching him and smiled as he gave her hand a gentle squeeze.

"I can't believe this is happening," she said.

"Things can change fast."

"I've talked with several colleagues about changing my name. Because I'm established in my field as Dr. Remington Chase, it makes sense to keep my name as it is in professional circles. But if I take your last name in our personal lives, it will just be confusing. I think it's best if I just keep my name as is."

"I agree."

"Phew. I was worried about that. Our children will be named Dawson." She smiled. "I wish we could get started on that."

Greer's face showed shock and pleasure. He didn't seem to find words to respond. "Seriously?"

She nodded. "I know it's not the best of times, but we should at least begin talking about it. Do you even want kids?"

Greer stared out the front windshield. "If you'd asked me that before we met, my answer would have been fuck no. But now, with you, I do. But then, I look at how much has changed just in the time that Ivy and Mandy have been expecting. Everything's upside-down." He gave her a quick look. "I don't want to put you and the baby in danger."

"We have some time. Let's see how things shake out."

They reached the county clerk's office. Remi's stomach was full of butterflies. Greer seemed as cool as ever. "Nervous?" she asked.

"Happy is more like it." He smiled and took her hand.

An hour later, they walked out with their marriage license. Remi took it out of the envelope and stared at it as they walked back to the SUV. "This makes it so real."

"Oh, it is real. It's happening. Do you want to go shopping for our rings?"

"Yes." She slipped her arms around Greer's waist. "I just want a simple gold band. No diamonds. Nothing fancy."

Greer frowned. "You sure?"

"Positive. The ring is my statement. I don't need to impress anyone with gemstones."

"Righto. Simple rings for us. We should be able to find that pretty easily."

The first jewelry store they went to didn't have rings in their sizes, and they didn't want to wait. The second store had a matching set that fit perfectly.

They went to lunch after that. Remi couldn't resist the temptation to open their ring boxes and stare at the simple rings. Both were narrow but heavy, so they felt more substantial than other slim gold bands.

She smiled at Greer. "I can't wait. We're starting our lives together."

He lifted her ring hand and kissed her knuckles. "I have a feeling that it's not going to be anything approaching a quiet life."

"That's okay. It'll be an adventure." Remi took a breath, worried about how to say what she had to tell him. "Would you be upset if I don't wear a wedding dress Saturday?"

"Yes." He stared at her, seriously affronted. "I'll be damned if the other guys on the team get to see you naked."

Remi laughed. "No. I mean, I don't want to wear the traditional garb for the ceremony. I did that once. The idea of putting some white wedding finery on makes me sweat."

"Oooh. You should have said that. I want you to wear what you want to wear. But, you know, Val is making arrangements with his friend to bring up choices. We better tell him what it is you're looking for so he doesn't waste time with the wrong options."

"I want to wear jeans and a fancy top. Maybe a sweater. I don't know. Just not a white or pastel dress. Not a dress at all. And sports coats for the guys. Or not. I don't care."

"My mom and sisters are going to be floored when Val brings the shopping to them."

"It's going to be such a fun day. Do you think Max can take your spot as DJ?"

"Or we can just bring one in," Greer said.

"Are we going to have a best man and maid of honor?"

"Absolutely. I want Max to stand up with me."

"I thought it would be nice if Ace, as your sister, was my maid of honor."

"My parents would love that. You think she will?"

"We'll find out. She's been doing a great job of stepping out of the shadows and being part of your family."

"*Our* family, now."

"Yeah. What do you think about my asking Owen if he'd walk me down the aisle?"

"That would make his day. For such a curmudgeon, he does seem to truly enjoy family stuff."

Their lunch was delivered. Remi was almost too excited to eat.

OWEN WAS in the den when Greer and Remi came in later that afternoon. For some reason that Remi couldn't identify, butterflies were racing around in her gut.

"Owen, I have a request to make," Remi said.

Owen's expression was reserved.

"I was wondering if you would walk me down the aisle. I know I could walk myself—I've ditched a lot of the wedding traditions for our ceremony—but I think I might like an arm to lean on."

"I'd be honored," Owen said, then looked at Greer. "I'll get her down that aisle one way or another, even if I have to throw her over my shoulder to deliver her."

"I don't think that will be necessary." Remi sounded ticked.

Greer chuckled. "If anyone's going to be carrying her, it's me."

"Oh, good grief." Remi spun on her heel and led Greer out of the room. So much testosterone. She couldn't even.

"You made him happy," Greer said. "He likes the dad role."

"He's not much older than you guys. Or me."

"Maybe not, but he takes being the boss seriously." Greer reached for her hand. "I'm off to ask Max to be my best man."

"Good. I'll get with Ace. I can't believe how fast this is all coming together!"

THE NEXT MORNING, when Remi and Greer went down for breakfast, the living room and dining room were buzzing with excited voices. People were chattering about the wedding, about their visit, about their plans for the day.

It was so different from the usual start of Remi's day. Greer kept odd hours, so she was often up and out the door before he was awake. It was nice having a morning with him.

Greer got a text. He read it, then looked up at her, his eyes filled with devastation. He texted a quick response. Everyone in the world that he loved was here in this house, safe. What could cause that look?

He nodded to her to follow him out of the room. They went into the wine room, the little closet wedged between the kitchen and the dining room.

"What is it?"

"Your mom's body has been released. I asked them to deliver it to the funeral home here in town."

Remi nodded. At last they would have her nearby. "Okay. That's good news, so why the worried look?"

"They discovered in their investigation that she'd been murdered."

Remi skipped so many breaths that the room began to spin. Greer caught her and pulled her close. She melted into him, taking his strength for her own. This was the outcome she'd feared, the one she secretly knew was the truth all along.

Greer was rubbing her back in slow strokes.

"Do they know who did it?" she asked, looking up at him.

He shook his head. "Looks like there were dozens of victims across several decades of burials out there. Their investigation is just beginning. It's going to take some work."

"It is devastating to learn my suspicions were correct, but I'm not sad that we have a funeral and a wedding to organize, Greer. Having my mom near has been a dream. I'd love to have her put to rest before our wedding, if possible."

"We can postpone the wedding. We don't have to do everything all at once."

"We're not postponing the wedding."

He smiled at her emphatic response.

"We don't know when we'll all be together again. I don't want us to miss this opportunity."

"Okay. Then we'll forge on. If it gets to be too much, come to me. We'll get each other through this."

"Are the Grummond deaths being investigated? Or swept under the carpet?"

"The FBI is all over them. Lobo is down there working the case. And you know Mayor Sullivan isn't going to be brushed off."

"I like her. She's fierce. I wish I could be there, see how the townspeople are taking the news. I bet there are some who believe that if the elders ordered these killings, then they must have been rightful deaths. Not even something like this will change their minds about the Society they once belonged to—and to which they're still loyal."

"I'll talk to Owen and see if I can offer Max and my services out to assist in the investigation. Regardless, we'll probably dig into it."

"That would be a relief. I know you'd get to the bottom of it. You have special helpers from the other side."

"Ghosts like justice. At least, my ghosts do."

THE CLOTHES CAME Wednesday—three vans of them. If alterations were needed, there needed to be time for them before final delivery on Friday. Besides, if any of the women couldn't find what they were hoping for, the vans would have to come back up tomorrow. When Greer announced the arrival, all the women hurried to the billiards room to see the new stuff.

Tina, Nancy, and Blithe stood with Ace and Remi as the apparel was rolled in on racks. Val was the only man allowed in the room, and he ran the operation like it was the most important show in his portfolio.

Nancy and Tina exchanged perplexed looks. Ace ignored them. So what if her boyfriend was not only an extraordinary and award-winning sniper, but was also into women and beauty and fashion?

She considered putting their questions to rest, but what did it really matter what anyone thought of anyone? Perhaps they thought she was naive and unworldly for not having the same concerns about his sexual orientation, but she knew exactly how he was oriented. She'd had more experience with men than all the women in the room put together, and from her perspective, Val was the perfect man.

Ace slipped her arms through her sisters' as they waited for him to oversee the arrangement of racks and dressing rooms and free-standing mirrors.

"How did he put this together?" Tina asked.

"Val has cultivated relationships with all kinds of shoppers and shopkeepers. We've had five weddings in the group already, so he's perfected his skills. Friday the manicurists and hairdressers are coming in. I think he's got masseuses scheduled for Thursday."

"That's it. I'm leaving Steve and moving in with you," Tina said.

Ace laughed. "Watch Val work with Remi. He has such an eye. He somehow finds what makes a woman glow from the inside out so that what she's wearing isn't mere adornment but actually shows off her inner beauty."

"You said he's the team's sniper? How can he be both?" Nancy asked.

"Because he can see evil as clearly as beauty."

REMI FELT a turbulent mix of pleasure and embarrassment at being the center of attention while Val pulled dresses off the racks and held them up to her. He didn't even ask if she liked something or not—as soon as he held it in front of her, he knew.

She was pleased that all of the clothes he brought in were secondhand. The extravagance of new clothes every time someone got married seemed excessive. And spending thousands of dollars for a one-day event was, in her pragmatic mind, the worst kind of overindulgence.

Val smiled at her. "One day to spoil yourself, to make extreme memories, cannot be bad."

She must have been frowning. "I just want casual."

Val stared at her so long that she thought he was going to nix her idea. "Good. Casual it is." He turned to the lead shopper. "Bring in the rest."

Her jaw dropped. She punched his arm. "You were testing me."

"Greer told me you wanted casual. But I figured a girl has a right to change her mind."

Remi laughed. A female bartender handed her a glass of champagne, then took the tray around to the other women. This was insane, but also so wonderful.

Val's Caribbean-blue eyes became serious. "I want you to be happy, Remi."

Her eyes watered. She fingered the locket she wore, wishing her mom were there with her, being spoiled. "You have no idea how happy I am, Val." She waved her hand around the room. "This lavish dress party is amazing."

"Good."

Several more racks were rolled into the room. They featured several different styles of kimonos, cardigans, pullovers, vests, and wraps, in wool, cashmere, mohair, satin, silk, and synthetic mixes, some understated, some overly vibrant. There were racks of jeans and shoes, a wide assortment of decorative hair pieces and jewelry.

"I know that these are consignments and pre-owned, but used haute couture is still out of reach of my professor's salary," she whispered to Val. "I looked at some of the price tags."

"Nonsense. Greer has this covered. His gift to you. And it's not all designer pieces. We'll find just the perfect ensemble."

"What if I don't want white? Or pastel? What if I want to go with something bold?"

"Your wedding. Your rules."

"I want something the Prophet would never have allowed."

"Screw the Prophet. Get something you love without any thoughts of him or the Grummonds. Make yourself happy—that's the best revenge."

11

The turnout for Remi's mom's funeral included the entire household. A black canopy had been set up over rows of black folding chairs. Remi was glad for the cover—it turned out to be a cold, rainy spring day, as if nature itself mourned. A pastor read from the Bible and gave a brief sermon.

It was all so surreal. She'd purchased the plot for her mom months ago in the hopes that this day would happen. She'd even had the headstone made. All that had been missing was her mom, and now everything was complete.

The mood among those gathered was somber, as she supposed it should be, but this was the day Remi had been anticipating a long time, so mixed in with the sorrow was joy.

Her mom was at last at peace.

After the ceremony, she and Greer stood in a receiving line, thanking everyone for attending. The pastor had come over to give his condolences. And then everyone but Greer was gone. The casket was still on its lift. Somewhere, employees were waiting to finish the burial and take down the canopy.

Life just marched on.

Greer said nothing as he stood by her side. She had in her hand a white calla lily that she'd taken from a vase at the corner of the grave. She couldn't quite bring herself to set it on the casket and walk away.

Long minutes passed. Greer said nothing and didn't move. At last, she looked at him. She knew he would wait as long as she needed...but she needed so much more time than she'd had.

"You promise she sees us?" Remi asked.

Greer nodded. "I promise."

"How can you know?"

"I've seen too much to not believe that."

She reached for his hand. "I don't know that I can process it all today."

"No one expects you to."

"Am I a bad person to want to be happy? She's back where she belongs. You and I are going to be married. I have a lot to be happy for."

"We both do."

Remi stepped closer to Greer. He was such a rock in her life, exactly what she needed to brave the storms the rest of her life would bring. She looked at him, hoping she could be his rock as well. "I love you."

He smiled, a minimalist gesture that showed the

depth of wisdom he'd already acquired. "I love you. Let's go give your mom the send-off she deserves."

She'd forgotten that Jim and Russ had stayed behind at Blade's to finish preparing an amazing feast in her mom's honor. Blade's place was home, especially with their friends and Greer's family all there.

It was the only home she'd ever really had.

IT WAS STILL dark outside when Greer woke Remi on their wedding day. "Good morning, my almost-wife."

Remi smiled and stretched, then wrapped her arms around his neck.

"I brought you some coffee," he said.

She pulled him under the covers, settling him between her legs. "Last time as our single selves—Dr. Chase and Mr. Dawson."

He laughed as he kissed her. "Right. Because after this morning, we'll be Dr. Chase and Mr. Dawson." He pushed her tank top up, lavishing attention on her breasts. She was still deliciously bed-warm. When he moved a hand down to push her pajama bottoms down, he realized she was naked from the waist down. He looked at her in surprise.

She giggled. "I heard you leave a few minutes ago. Thought I'd surprise you."

He pushed up to his knees, then shoved his underwear and flannel pajama bottoms down before settling between her legs and entering her.

She pulled the covers up over him. "This is how we should start every morning. Sex and coffee."

"Agreed. We'll put that in our vows."

"No. We'll just keep it as our secret promise to each other."

"Until we have kids…"

She caught his face, but closed her eyes as her body took over her ability to think. They found their release almost simultaneously. Remi looked up at him, her eyes soft in the dim light he'd left on in the bathroom. "This week has been a dream. So much has happened. I love your family."

"Our family now."

"Yep. They are the best ever."

"I have something else for you," Greer said. He straightened his pajama bottoms, then went over to one of his drawers in their dresser and pulled out a bag from a jeweler in Denver. Sitting on the edge of the bed, he handed it to her.

She sat up and opened it. A little black jeweler's box was inside. Greer reached over to flip the light on the nightstand on. She cracked the box open. Inside, resting on a sloping shelf of black velvet, was a pair of ruby-and-diamond earrings.

"You wouldn't let me get you a fancy ring, but I thought you could wear these now and then."

Her eyes were huge. Her mouth was frozen in a big O.

"Say something."

"I love them. They're gorgeous."

"You should know both the diamonds and the rubies were lab-grown, so no negative environmental impacts occurred in creating them."

Remi held the box close to her chest and shook her head. "You already know me so well. Why the rubies?"

Greer looked at the earrings. Square-cut diamonds were mounted above large, red, teardrop rubies, all in an eighteen-karat yellow-gold setting with a special rear clasp. "The blood red reminded me of life, the very thing you study. People lost, saved, all of us trying to become more than we are now. I know that you are always aware of the delicate dance we do to get through life with our hearts intact. When you wear these, you'll remind me of that."

Remi put the earrings on, then leaned over and hugged him. "My gift for you isn't nearly as grand, but it does come with an interesting story."

Greer rubbed his hands together. "I love stories."

Remi pulled her pajama bottoms on, then reached over to her nightstand and took out a beat-up blue jewelry box that was wide and flat. She held the box, looking at it. "I was in town with Jim earlier this week, helping him with food shopping for after the funeral. I hadn't decided what to get you for your wedding present yet. I didn't want to rush it, so I was thinking it would have to wait until after we were married. But while I was in town, I had the strangest urge to go into the thrift store down the street. There was an old man at the front desk, trying to hawk his watch. For some reason, maybe because he looked so in need, maybe because he was so sad at having to give up his watch, I don't know, I just needed to see it.

"It was beautiful. The shop couldn't afford the amount he was asking. He said it was solid fourteen-karat gold and had been given to him by his wife, who died a long time ago. I offered to buy it from him on the spot. He accepted. I went to the store's ATM and paid him cash. Then I bought a new leather band." She held the box to her chest as she'd done with her gift. "I hope you like it. There is an inscription in the back, but the shopkeeper said that could be buffed out and a new one inscribed." She handed him the box. He could feel her nervousness.

When he opened the box, he stared at the gold watch with its battered black leather band, feeling the blood leave his face. He turned the watch over and read the inscription.

"'To H.G. Myers from Bethany. This is your ticket home to me.'"

He threw it on the bed then jumped back, staring at it. He shook his head.

Remi gasped. "You hate it. Oh, God. I'm so sorry." She tossed the covers over the watch, hiding it from him.

"No." Greer shook his head. "No. No, I don't hate it." He took a calming breath. "Tell me again, every-thing, exactly as it happened."

She did.

"What did he look like?"

She shook her head. "An old guy. Your height. Graying dark hair. Blue eyes. Bushy gray brows."

"No beard?"

"No. Clean-shaven. Do you think he cheated me? Is it not gold?"

"Remi—this watch was my grandfather's. Bethany was my grandmother. This was a standing joke between them. When he worked for the CIA, she was always worried he'd get stranded somewhere. She said there was enough gold in there to get him home, that she'd rather him than the watch."

"How is that possible?" She frowned. "What kind of coincidence would bring it to town now, just in time for our wedding?"

Greer shook his head. "This watch was missing from his things when he died. We never knew what happened to it."

"Greer, did I see your grandfather's ghost?"

"I don't know."

"Is it a cursed watch?"

"No." He looked at her, still feeling stricken. "It's just, sort of, a miracle." He went over to her and drew her off the bed so that he could hug her. "Thank you. Thank you so much. I love it."

"Henry was Santo, wasn't he?"

"Yeah. He trained Ace and me. He trained the Legion, too."

"Didn't you think he faked his death?"

Greer nodded. "That's what the Legion thinks."

There was a knock on their door. "You guys decent?" Ace asked through the door.

"No," Greer said. "Give us ten. We need showers."

"Right—showers. Do it in five. We have a wedding to get ready for!"

"Fifteen minutes, and the room's yours."

"I don't need the room. I need Remi. Her stuff's all in Addy's suite downstairs. And you have fourteen minutes left, so get moving."

Greer grinned at Remi. "The day's starting." He pulled her into his arms and kissed her.

"It sure is. We better get that shower done. Ace can be scary when she's mad."

GREER KISSED Remi goodbye after their showers. When she was out of the room, he quickly got ready. There was something he had to do before the ceremony. He pocketed Santo's watch, then took the backstairs to the first floor and went down to the bunker from the den.

When he walked into the ops room, Max looked up at him. "'Sup? You're not supposed to be here—today of all days." Greer took the watch box from his pocket and opened it. Max whistled. "Sweet. You need help getting the new band on?"

"No."

Max went still. "Fuck. Me. What is it?"

"This is Santo's watch. Remi bought it from an old

guy at the thrift store." Greer told Max what Remi had said about buying the watch.

"You think Santo's in town?"

"No idea. I thought I'd get whatever fingerprints I can recover. Then, after the ceremony, I'm giving the watch to you to take apart. If Santo pushed this on her, there had to be a reason."

Max's eyes narrowed. "You think Santo's still alive? I know the Legion seems to think so, but his body was turned in to the FBI after his fight with Ace."

"And then it disappeared, so who knows."

"I'll tell Owen. He can relay the info to Liege."

"Good." Greer was already sitting at his desk, running the watch, its band, the replacement band, and the case under the software lens that grabbed fingerprints. The watch was wiped clean of all prints except Remi's. Same with the original band. The new band and the case had Remi's prints, an unknown set that the system was doing a search on...and a set of smudges that had no identifying markers.

He looked over at Max, who was watching the data come up on the computer screen. "What the hell is that?"

"We could never get Bastion's prints, could we?" Greer asked.

"No."

"Do mutants lose their fingerprints in the mutation process?"

"Let's have Owen ask Liege."

"Have me ask what?" Owen said as he came into the ops room.

Greer brought him up to speed.

"If Santo is here, Liege needs to know." Owen made the call. The two leaders spoke briefly, then Owen hung up. "He said Guerre's already on his way over to provide backup security for the wedding. He'll check things out while he's here. I guess several options are possible. The man Remi bought it from was a messenger. Or he was Santo in disguise. Or the whole thing was an implanted memory."

"But how would Remi have gotten the actual watch if it was a false memory? And who did she give her payment to?" Greer asked.

"Santo could have left the watch here months ago," Owen said, "told her where and when to find it, then activated the false memory. We know Santo was changed more than a decade ago. The things these modified humans can do boggles the mind. Liege did say that Guerre is able to read energy left on inanimate objects, that we should let him have a look at the watch."

Greer nodded. "Sure. I just need to wear it for the ceremony, so any time before or after that."

Owen's gaze bounced between Greer and Max. "And the answer to your other question is yes—some mutants do lose their finger and toe prints."

12

R emi looked through the mirror she was sitting
in front of to the group of women gathered
behind her. They looked happy. She remembered the day she'd been forced to marry Prophet
Josiah, while she and her mother were still part of the
Grummond Society. She was twelve and terrified—as
were all the other girls he was marrying that day. Even
her mother was unhappy about the situation.

Everything about that day was sick and forced and
twisted.

Today was the exact opposite—fun, celebratory, and
joyful.

Addy was watching Ace work magic on Remi's hair,
braiding and rolling and pinning it in a complicated
confection. Remi looked at Ace's hands. She'd been one
of the Omni attendants who'd prepped Addy for her
forced marriage to Cecil Edwards. Ace had the soul of
an artist and the heart of a warrior. Remi was glad she

was finding a way for the disparate parts of her spirit to work together.

"Everyone decent?" Val asked before he turned the corner into the sitting room outside Owen's suite of bedrooms.

"You're clear," Ace called out, her words muffled from the bobby pins in her mouth.

Val came into the sitting room. He was holding a tray of mimosas. The photographer that Ace had hired for her brother's wedding stepped around him and began snapping pictures of the women with Remi.

"We've been all over the house, capturing the images on your list," he said, smiling at Ace. "We caught the men hanging out together, the kids tying their ties, the visiting family members, the beautiful wedding hall. I think we should talk Owen into renting this place out for weddings and events."

Ace huffed a laugh that sent a whisper of air across Remi's neck. She straightened and looked at her work. Addy brought over a tray of baby's-breath and miniature ruby-red roses for Ace to pin into Remi's hair. The petite arrangements matched the earrings that Greer had given Remi. Ace must have coordinated with him.

Everyone had done so much work in such a short time on her and Greer's behalf over the last week. Remi had been distracted by her mom's funeral and ceremony. If the wedding had been left to her, she would have rolled out of bed, showered, put any old thing on, and then gone down to meet the justice of the peace. But thanks to the huge group effort, her wedding had turned into a magical event.

Val had brought the manicurists in yesterday, so all the females, in and attending the wedding, had fresh nails. He'd even insisted that Greer and Max get their own manicures. Remi grinned, thinking she'd laugh about that for a long time.

Ivy and Eddie were out on the basketball court over-seeing its transformation into that wedding hall that Val talked about. Eddie was doing Ivy's bidding—the back and forth from the kitchen to the gym building was too much running around for Ivy's advanced pregnancy. She and Mandy had been parked in comfortable chairs from which they could oversee operations.

Val gave Remi the rundown: the caterers had arrived with their brunch buffet; the bakery had delivered the wedding cake and other sweet confections; the DJ was setting up his equipment; the justice of the peace was downstairs.

Everything was ready.

Remi stood up and looked around the room, ignoring the flash and snapping of the photographer. Ace gave her a hand mirror so that she could see the back of her head. "Ace, you're missing your calling. You're a sculptor. This is stunning!"

Ace cracked her knuckles. "Glad I can put my skills to work for good instead of evil."

A look of confusion flitted across Blithe's face. Remi was glad she didn't question what Ace had meant by that. There was clearly a lot more work that needed to be done between mother and daughter, but Remi hoped that would come with time. For now, Blithe seemed to accept that there was a lot she didn't —and possibly wouldn't—know about her youngest daughter.

Remi took one last look at herself in the mirror. Her outfit was beautiful and elegant, definitely something she'd wear again on special occasions with Greer.

Her pants were slim-fitting, high-rise, raspberry-colored velvet jeans. Her cream satin, cowl-neck camisole was only tucked into her pants in the middle of her waist, exposing a wide, tan leather belt. Over the camisole, she wore a filmy silk Shibori jacket that came just to her hips. The tissue-thin material had a gradient color that went from yellow to orange to rose at the bottom, ending with the same color as her pants. The shoes she wore were shimmering golden stilettos with an ankle strap.

Her mom's locket was the only thing she wore around her neck, complementing the simple lines of her outfit.

She turned and smiled at Val. "We did good picking this out."

"Oh yeah, we did. The Grummonds would kick you out for just wearing that, never mind getting married in it."

"Mission accomplished." And best of all, she felt beautiful.

"Come stand in the middle of the room here so we can get pictures of you," the photographer said. "First you alone, then with your maid of honor. Then with your family, then with your friends."

The next few minutes passed quickly in a blur of different poses and groupings. Just before the friend pictures, Fiona rushed in wearing skinny blue jeans, a pastel peasant top, and yellow flats.

"You're here!" Remi said, reaching for a hug.

Fiona laughed. "I made it! This is so exciting. I'm sorry I missed everything this week." She looked at her outfit. "Especially the shopping. But Val did great finding something fresh for me."

Ace shook her head. "The man's a women's-clothing savant."

Fiona hugged Ace and said, "He is—thank you for sharing him." She gave Remi another big hug. "I'm so happy for you. These days are so much fun—I wish I'd been here the whole week. And I'm sorry to hear about your mom."

Remi nodded. "She's where she needs to be now, safe while the investigation into her death is ongoing." Remi looked at Greer's mom and sisters. "Everybody, this is Fiona. Fee, this is Greer's mom Blithe, and his sisters, Tina and Nancy." Fee shook hands with them, then hugged Hope, Addy, Ace, and Val. "Where is everyone?"

"Ivy, Mandy, and Eden are downstairs managing the event. Wynn is handling the kids," Ace said.

Remi smiled at her. "We run these things like clock-work now."

"And that's how it should be," Owen said as he came into the sitting room.

Seeing him, Remi's stomach knotted. This was really happening. She'd said that so many times, but it still seemed unreal.

"You look beautiful," Owen told Remi. He sent a glance around the room. "All of you do."

Remi reached for Ace's hand and squeezed it. The outfit she wore was classic...for Ace. Black faux-leather leggings and a black linen tank top with elaborate and colorful beadwork and embroidery in the shape of flowers and geometric patterns. She wore her black combat boots with the steel buckles. And she'd redone her ombre in a fuchsia color that would complement what Remi wore. She looked fierce and feminine at the same time. Best of all, what she wore wasn't something the Grummonds would ever have allowed a female to wear, especially not as a wedding attendant.

"Are you ready?" Owen asked Remi.

She nodded. "Is the JP set up?"

"He is."

"I guess we should all go on to our seats," Blithe said. Tina and Nancy paused to give Remi and Ace hugs. Blithe held Remi's arms and stared into her eyes. "It's an honor to have you join our family, honey. Reed and I already love you as one of our own."

Remi sucked in a ragged breath.

"Don't you dare make her cry, Mom," Ace said. "I just spent hours on getting her ready!"

Blithe gave Ace a stunned look. Remi knew it was

because Ace publicly called her "Mom." Remi grabbed both women into a hug. This was the best day ever.

Ace picked up Remi's bouquet from a dry vase and handed it to her. It was a beautiful collection of pastel roses in yellow, orange, red, and fuchsia, colors that echoed those in the short silk kimono top Remi wore.

Addy pinned a white rose boutonnière into Owen's lapel. His eyes were serious as he watched her. When she was finished, she smiled up at him and smoothed the jacket over his chest.

That was love. And a lifetime of that would start in just minutes for Remi and Greer.

Hope and Fiona drew Val and the women away as they led the group out to the gym wing, leaving her alone with Owen and the photographer.

He handed a tissue to Remi. "Just dab, like this," he said, mimicking the motion of light touches on his face.

Remi laughed. "How do you know that?"

"From watching Addy."

Remi tucked the tissue into her pocket. She straightened her shoulders, sniffed, then nodded at him.

Owen was watching her with a serious expression. "You're joining your life with a good man. I wish you a long and joyful marriage."

"Dammit." Remi retrieved the tissue and dabbed at her face.

"Sorry." He held out his arm. "Let's do this."

Remi was glad she had him by her side. She was so happy that she thought without him she might just float the whole way down to Greer.

They walked quickly to the gym wing. Angel and Blade were standing at the entrance to the basketball court. They both hugged Remi and gave her their good wishes. Then they opened the doors. Everyone inside stood up and turned to face them as the music announced their arrival.

Owen bent close and said, "We go slow here."

His soft comment, from a man who so rarely was gentle with his people, sent another wave of emotion through her. She nodded at him, then they stepped inside the room.

Remi felt dizzy.

Split between two aisles were her Red Team family, Greer's family, and the dozens of kids from both sides, all of them smiling with joy, some even fighting happy tears.

Max was standing straight and tall. His often-severe expression softened as he watched her come toward his best friend. His happy face was almost more unnerving than his threatening one.

Remi's eyes sought Greer's. He didn't smile, but his somber expression filled her with strength and warmth. Her bouquet kept her from fingering her mother's locket, but she knew her mom was there in spirit.

When Owen came even with Greer, he gave her a kiss on the cheek and handed her off, then took his seat next to Addy.

Remi handed her bouquet to Ace, then took Greer's hands. He kissed her cheek, then said, "I love you. Are you ready for this?"

"I love you too. And I was ready for this forever ago."

"Good." He nodded at the justice of the peace.

"Let us begin." The JP, who had officiated several of the Red Team weddings, gave a brief, lovely lecture on the meaning of marriage. It set the tone perfectly for the exchange of their vows.

Remi looked into Greer's amber eyes. The room full of people slipped from her mind; she knew they were there as witnesses to the ceremony, so she spoke loudly and clearly, but her words were meant only for Greer.

"Greer, life with you has been full of adventure already, and I know we're only at the beginning of our journey. Your courage and lighthearted nature attracted me to you right away. Your vision, ethics, and huge capacity for love already light my way. I love you more than I can put into words, but I will happily spend the rest of my life giving you the joy you give me."

Greer smiled at her and kissed her forehead. "Remi, you are everything I never thought I'd get to experience in my life. I love your fierce belief in humanity—something I often think I lost a long time ago. The hope and love you so openly give those around you lights my way in dark and wonderful times alike. I, too, will happily spend the rest of my life giving you the joy you give me."

Remi smiled at Greer, trying to stay somber, when all she wanted to do was scream and jump and laugh. He slipped her simple gold band on her finger. She put his on him. The JP pronounced them man and wife and invited them to share their first kiss.

Greer leaned over and wrapped his arms around her waist, lifting her off the ground for a passionate kiss.

When he set her back on her feet, Ace gave her the bouquet back. The JP introduced them to their friends and invited them up to congratulate them.

Greer kissed Remi seconds before they were swarmed. "I love you, Dr. Chase."

"I love you, Mr. Dawson."

13

The lights behind the house caught the swirling mist, lifting it out of the inky blackness. Greer found himself drawn toward something in the lower lawn. This felt so real, but then he realized he wasn't cold, even though he hadn't worn his coat. In fact, he seemed to move without actually walking.

This had to be a dream.

He moved toward the far edge of the yard, nearing the woods that bordered it. A man appeared seemingly from nowhere. Long white hair and beard. Loose white garments.

Santo.

Grandpa Henry.

Greer stopped moving forward. The guy looked so real. But Ace had been certain she'd killed him in their last fight at the White Kingdom Brotherhood's compound months ago. Yet there he stood.

Maybe he was a ghost.

What does it matter what I am? his grandfather asked, speaking without moving his lips.

"Are you a ghost?"

Maybe.

"Why are you here?"

I didn't want to miss your wedding.

"Like you fucking cared about any other event in my life."

I cared about all of them.

Greer shook his head. "No. I've come to understand that you only cared about what furthered your objectives."

It's true, that was a priority. But then I knew you and Ace were extraordinary—you were more than capable of meeting the challenges you would face in this life.

It was shameful how impactful those words were to Greer. As a kid, starting his training so damn young, he had lived to please his grandfather.

You always did please me.

"I can't say the same for you."

One day, Greer, you'll live far longer than you should have, and you'll see life with the eyes of an old man. I pray you reach that level of wisdom.

Greer bit his tongue. He didn't know what that meant, but did know he was a long way from understanding it.

Santo turned to go into the woods. Greer felt a crushing sadness, as if he was losing his grandfather all over again. He loved him as much as he hated him, and all of it was torture. "Thank you for your watch."

Santo paused and looked back. He smiled at Greer. *Take the changes, my boy. Accept the future that belongs to you. It's your ticket home.*

OTHER BOOKS BY ELAINE LEVINE

O-MEN: LIEGE'S LEGION

PARANORMAL SUSPENSE

LIEGE

BASTION

RED TEAM SERIES

ROMANTIC SUSPENSE/MILITARY SUSPENSE

(This series must be read in order.)

1 THE EDGE OF COURAGE

2 SHATTERED VALOR

3 HONOR UNRAVELED

4 KIT & IVY: A RED TEAM WEDDING NOVELLA

5 TWISTED MERCY

6 TY & EDEN: A RED TEAM WEDDING NOVELLA

7 ASSASSIN'S PROMISE

8 WAR BRINGER

9 ROCCO & MANDY: A RED TEAM WEDDING NOVELLA

10 RAZED GLORY

11 DEADLY CREED

12 FORSAKEN DUTY

13 MAX & HOPE: A RED TEAM WEDDING NOVELLA

14 Owen & Addy: A Red Team Wedding Novella

15 Greer & Remi: A Red Team Wedding Novella

16 angel & Wynn: A Red Team Wedding Novella

Sleeper SEALs

Romantic Suspense/Military Suspense

11 Freedom Code

Men of Defiance Series

Historical Western Romance

(This series may be read in any order.)

1 Rachel and the Hired Gun

2 Audrey and the Maverick

3 Leah and the Bounty Hunter

4 Logan's Outlaw

5 Agnes and the Renegade

ABOUT THE AUTHOR

Elaine Levine has a simple life and a twisted mind, both of which need constant care and feeding. She writes in several different subgenres of romance, including romantic suspense/military, historical western, and paranormal suspense. Her books are sexy, edgy, and suspenseful, but always end on a happy note because she believes love gives everything meaning.

Be sure to sign up for her new release announcements at http://geni.us/GAlUjx.

If you enjoyed this book, please consider leaving a review at your favorite online retailer and Goodreads to help other readers find it.

Get social! Connect with Elaine online:
>   Reader Group: http://geni.us/2w5d
>   Website: https://www.ElaineLevine.com
>   email: elevine@elainelevine.com

Made in the USA
San Bernardino, CA
19 November 2019